Unseen Hope

C. Frederic Smith

Unseen Hope by C. Frederic Smith
Copyright ©2025 by Smith Endeavors LLC
All rights reserved. This book is protected under the copyright laws of the United States of America. This book may not be copied or reprinted for commercial gain or profit.

Scripture quotations are taken from the HOLY BIBLE, New International Version®, NIV® Copyright© 1973, 1978, 1984, 2011 by Biblica, Inc.® unless otherwise noted. Used by permission. All rights reserved worldwide.

Scripture marked MSG is taken from THE MESSAGE. Copyright© 1993, 1994, 1995, 1996, 2000, 2001, 2002. Used by permission of NavPress Publishing Group.

ISBN 978-1-956365-88-7 (print)
ISBN 978-1-956365-89-4 (e-book)

For Worldwide Distribution
Printed in the U.S.A.

River Birch Press
P.O. Box 7341, Mesa, AZ 85216

ACKNOWLEDGMENTS

There are many acknowledgments I need to make in this attempt at generating creative work. First, I thank God and my Lord and Savior, Jesus Christ, for this unique opportunity in my life.

I am very blessed with my wife, Martha, whose support cannot be quantified! She has been very supportive of my past endeavors; most noteworthy is my completing a Ph.D. in Aeronautics and Astronautics while I was working full-time and with three young children.

I am grateful for Martha and my children, their spouses, and our grandchildren, who always remind us of what being a family means. I am forever indebted to my parents, Crawford and Barbara Smith, who both grew up in the Great Depression. My dad was also a World War II veteran. They both taught me the value of hard work and the importance of family.

Finally, but not least, I thank my many church pastors who provided insights into scriptures over the years.

PREFACE

My life took an unexpected turn on Friday, January 23, 2015. A routine colonoscopy resulted in the need to have a benign polyp removed surgically due to it being too large to remove during the procedure. The surgery was done on Wednesday, February 4, and I spent the next six weeks at home recovering. I thanked God for the good outcome and prayed that the Holy Spirit would tell me how to live the rest of my life in serving God as I felt I was given a new opportunity to evaluate my purpose on earth.

I believe part of an answer to my prayer came on the following Monday. I was reading my daily devotion and was inspired by Psalm 102:18, "Let this be written for a future generation, that a people not yet created may praise the Lord." The devotional writer asked what we are writing today that may inspire future generations to praise the Lord. That is the inspiration for this book.

—*Fred Smith*

*Now faith is confidence
in what we hope for
and assurance about what
we do not see*
(HEBREWS 11:1).

ONE

"Elizabeth, we need to talk," Christopher Baldwin said to Elizabeth, his ex-wife and mother of their three children—John, Sarah, and Jennifer—after she opened the door at his former home.

"Sure. What's on your mind?" she asked with a concerned look. "Come on in."

Christopher and Elizabeth sat down together on a couch in the living room.

"I have some news to share with you and the kids but wanted to discuss this with you first. I have decided to take a job in Los Angeles."

"Why are you deciding to leave Chicago? The kids are here, and you won't be able to see them very often," Elizabeth said with a look of shock on her face.

"I know this is a surprise to you. My current job is getting to be a dead-end position with no future advancement opportunities. This new job is a vice-presidential position with significant upward potential," he replied with a matter-of-fact tone in his voice.

"You make a great income here, and the kids enjoy seeing you regularly. Do you understand what this will do to them?"

"I have considered this, and I am sure they will be OK with it over time. Initially, I agree it may be upsetting to them. However, they have adjusted to our divorce, and I'm sure they'll also adjust to my not being here regularly. They have their own friends, and I'm not sure how important it is to them that I am in the area."

"Although we have obviously had our differences, you're still their father, and I believe you can still play an important role in their lives," Elizabeth replied with a determined tone. "Why is it so important for you to take this job? Life is not all about work. In fact, your family should be more important than work. When you die, will your legacy be about work or those you live life with including your family and friends?"

"I think you're getting much too philosophical about this. We're just talking about a job and career opportunities, not eternity!" Christopher said with exasperation.

"Maybe we are, and maybe we aren't. All I'm saying is if you leave Chicago for Los Angeles, you'll lose touch with your children."

"Look, I'll call weekly and travel back here often. They may enjoy visiting me in LA sometimes. It would be a great place to spend winter break, away from the cold weather here."

"I don't think being a part-time and commuting parent is a very good substitute for being present all the time."

"I'm surprised you think so highly of me as a parent, considering we could not stay married," Christopher said confused.

"We have our differences, and to be honest, perhaps we didn't work hard enough to resolve them," she replied. "But the past cannot be changed. However, I think you still can play a positive role in our children's lives."

"I agree that what is done is done. When we were married, no one wanted to leave Chicago when I had job opportunities elsewhere. Now that we're divorced, I can move and get what I want, and the kids can stay here with you and get what you want."

"So, this is just a business transaction for you! I can't believe the family means so little to you. You know what, I'll tell the kids about your leaving, and you can just go now and get on with your life!" she yelled at him.

Christopher was surprised at her reaction, which he had not ever previously experienced. However, he decided it was best if he left and let her tell the children the news.

TWO

The cell phone alarm went off at 5:30 AM. Christopher touched the snooze choice as he stared at the ceiling, thinking about his day ahead. He had a critical meeting with a major client. This was one of several that he had brought into the company since he joined a few years ago. His life was so much different now. He was at the top of his game with no distractions except for one. His girlfriend, Candace, was half his age at twenty-five and fun to be with. They had planned their usual date this evening. He didn't often think about his ex-wife, Elizabeth, or his three children, John, Sarah, and Jennifer. Occasionally, he called them out of feeling a deep-down obligation.

I better get up and take a shower to wake me up! I got a long day ahead of me, he thought. Before shaving and taking a shower, he checked his personal email on his cell phone. He also checked on how his investments were doing. The markets on the east coast would be opening soon.

After his shower, he had a couple of pieces of toast with slices of sharp cheddar cheese that made a sandwich out of it. He smiled as he remembered his grandfather eating this at breakfast when he was a kid. He also had a cup of coffee and orange juice.

He headed for the garage to start his hour-long drive to downtown Los Angeles. Although the drive to work was long, he enjoyed the quiet time in his luxury SUV. He usually listened to the news on one of the channels on satellite radio. Before his divorce, he lived in Chicago with his family. He liked living on central time with the local news at 10 PM, being only an hour behind the east coast where a significant amount of the national news occurs. Now, living in California, much has happened before he gets up in the morning, since it was three hours behind the eastern time zone.

He arrived at work at 8 AM. He parked in his reserved spot and took the elevator to the floor where the executive offices are found. He was the vice president of business development, which was a big step up from his prior position in Chicago. After his divorce, he felt free at last to pursue job opportunities outside of the Chicago area. Before his divorce, his wife and children would never agree to leave their home and friends in Chicago. Although they lived an extremely comfortable life, it was never enough for him. He always wanted more, no matter how successful he was.

He greeted his personal administrative assistant, Alicia, whose desk was just outside of his office. Settling into his chair, he looked at his calendar for the day and then checked his email. Most of it could wait, except for one from his boss, Don, the president of the company. He wanted to see him as soon as possible.

Great! An urgent message from your boss to see him as soon as possible was usually not good news. I've been working so hard here, giving 110% to the job. Outside of seeing Candace, I have no other personal life. It's just work and Candace. I must admit for most guys, Candace is enough to manage after work! he thought with a smirk.

He decided to head for Don's office right away. Don is a bit of a control freak and does not like to be kept waiting. His approach to attending meetings is if you're early, you're on time, and you're late if you arrive on time.

"Hi, Susan. Is Don available? I got a message that he wants to see me as soon as possible. I assume it's bad news."

"Don't be too sure of that," she replied with a smile. "I'll let Don know you're here."

"Hello, Chris. Have a seat," Don greeted Chris at the door and patted him on the shoulder.

"I know you have only been here a few years, but you have made an enormous impact on the company," Don began. "You have brought in five major accounts, more than others who have been much longer!"

Chris was not sure where the conversation was going. *At least it doesn't sound like I'll be fired*, he thought with a silent sigh of relief.

"You give your all for the company," Don continued. "You're one of our most dedicated employees. So, I want to let you know that you are on the short list for the next executive vice president position."

"That's incredible! Thank you very much for the opportunity," Chris replied with a surprised look.

"No thanks necessary—you earned it. If it was just up to me, I would promote you now. However, the board of directors wants to consider a few candidates. I think if you close the deal on your upcoming European trip, you'll seal the deal. I have every confidence that you can do it," Don declared.

"I'm looking forward to the trip. I have worked a lot of extra hours at night and on weekends getting ready for it," Chris said.

"I know you put in a lot of hours, and I want to reward you for your efforts and sacrifice. It's people like you and me that know how to keep our priorities straight. Many employees here and elsewhere don't put their career first and let a lot of personal matters distract them. I always say that if you put work first, the rest will take care of itself."

"Since coming out here, I have put all I can into my job. I appreciate being recognized."

"Well, just keep on doing what you're doing, and we'll take care of you," Don told him as he walked him to the door. "Have a great day!"

"You too, sir."

"So how did your meeting go?" Susan asked Chris as he was leaving.

"Great!" he said with a large smile.

I can't believe this. I thought I was in trouble, but instead, I'm being considered for a major promotion! I can't wait to tell Candace. I know she'll be impressed. Although I feel comfortable in my relationship with her, being twice her age always makes me wonder about the competition with those young guys, he thought.

Chris met his clients at 9:45 AM at the receptionist's desk to check them in and issue them visitor badges. They settled into the conference room ahead of schedule, just as Chris' manager Don would do to be considered on time. The clients took their seats on one side of the long table and Chris' team sat on the other side.

After introductions among all the attendees, the team leader for the client's team began the discussion. "We're concerned about your company meeting the schedule. I know there have been delays with your supply chain and so the delivery schedules are moving," she started the discussion.

"You're right about the problems we're having," Chris replied with a concerned look.

"Well, if this continues much longer, we may need to reconsider our contract. It does have a clause about meeting delivery schedules," she quickly said, barely letting Chris complete his thought.

Chris knew she was serious and not sure what to say. If he lost the contract, that would kill his chances at the promotion.

What can I do or say? he wondered. *If I tell them the truth and say we have no idea when this issue will be resolved, they will cancel the contract. I need to say whatever it takes to keep them on contract. I guess my only option is to lie and hope for the best.*

Chris decided to tell the other team that he had everything under control.

"Look, I know we're behind schedule right now, but I assure you that I have discussed the situation with the supplier, and they told me that they will get back on schedule very soon," Chris told them with a sincere tone. After misleading other clients several times, Chris had gotten good at making a convincing story in place of the truth.

"They better be back on schedule within the next two months, or we will cancel the contract," the leader replied skeptically.

That's great. I should have that promotion by then, so if things don't work out, who cares? Chris thought.

They went on to review the overall schedule and discuss other concerns for about an hour. Then Chris escorted them to the same reception area they arrived at, collected their visitor badges, and signed them out.

I'm glad that's over! Hopefully, the supplier will be back on schedule. Although I don't know that right now, it certainly could happen in two months. So, I really didn't lie, I just stretched the truth a bit, Chris thought. *I'm sure my boss wouldn't mind my stretching the truth a little to keep the client's business.*

THREE

Chris returned to his office and checked his calendar. He saw that he had lunch scheduled with his friend and a meeting with another vice president at the company. He also had a physical scheduled for later in the afternoon. He turned fifty recently, and his doctor said he should start yearly physicals. He already had his blood work done last week so he didn't have to fast before his appointment.

Chris met Sam at the usual restaurant. After ordering lunch, Chris talked about his morning.

"I can't believe how my meeting went this morning! The client was about to walk on me, and I stretched the truth a little bit to keep them under contract," Chris said to Sam.

"I got to admit I have done that occasionally over the years. I also admit I am not proud about it," Sam said with a guilty look.

"Hey, you just did what you needed to get things done. Everyone does it occasionally. It's just part of the culture," Chris replied firmly.

"So how are things with Candace?" Sam asked.

"Great! I feel so young when I'm around her. I really don't feel like I'm fifty then. When we're out, I wonder if people think she's my daughter! She's much more mature than her twenty-five years. She's focused on her career and not interested in having kids. The three from my last marriage are enough for me!"

"How are your kids doing in Chicago?" Sam asked.

"I think they're doing OK. I haven't talked with them lately. Maybe I should call soon," Chris said as he wondered when he last spoke with them.

"Do you think you should call more regularly?"

"I guess I should. You know how it is with work keeping me so busy. By the time I get done with work and get home after seeing Candace, it's late in Chicago with the two-hour time difference."

"I don't know how I would manage being far away from my kids," Sam told Chris.

"You get used to it after a while, Sam. Besides, there's so much to do in California, and my job opportunities here are so much better than I had in Chicago."

"You know your job isn't your life," Sam reminded Chris.

"I agree. I have Candace to keep me from being a work-a-holic!"

"I have an appointment for a physical with my doctor late today," Chris told Sam as he moved around uneasily in his seat, wanting to change the subject.

"That's right. You turned fifty a few weeks ago. I'll be fifty in a couple of years. I hear annual physicals are the routine then, not to mention the dreaded colonoscopy!" Sam said sarcastically.

"Hey, I got my trip to Europe coming up, and all that other stuff can wait."

"I forgot about your upcoming trip. How's that going?"

"This morning Don told me that I should get the promotion to executive VP if I have a successful European trip and close the deal."

"That's great news! I heard a rumor that there was a short list for the job. I'm sure I'm not on it. I just can't put enough time in at work. The kids and home keep me busy."

"That's one thing I don't have to deal with anymore. Families can get in the way of career advancement," Chris told Sam.

"I agree, but I wouldn't change a thing. I used to be more into my job but as the kids have gotten older, I find I enjoy spending time with them and my wife."

"I guess there are two views of work. Speaking of work, I must get back for a meeting," Chris said as they paid the check. As he quickly walked back to the office, he started to feel extremely uncomfortable with the conversation.

FOUR

After a couple of afternoon meetings, Chris left work for his doctor's appointment. Since his doctor's office was in Valencia, he allowed extra time to deal with the heavy traffic that always seemed to be there. He arrived at the doctor's office and checked in with the receptionist. He presented his insurance card. As a part of the paperwork, he was asked who could have access to his medical information. He realized he had always had his ex-wife Elizabeth listed in the past. After he thought about it briefly, he put his girlfriend Candace Parker down. He was not sure what that said about his relationship with her. After completing the forms, he sat down and waited to be called.

After about ten minutes, a nurse called his name. He got weighed and was shown to a small examination room. The nurse took his blood pressure, pulse, and temperature. She asked if he was taking any medications and if he had any allergies to medications. After this, she told him the doctor would see him shortly. Chris sat there and checked his cell phone for any email. After about five minutes there was a knock on the door, and Dr. Jones entered the room.

"Hi Chris. How are you doing today?"

"Fine. I turned fifty recently and as you recommended, I came in for a full physical."

"I'm glad you followed my recommendation. It's important that you start to pay closer attention to your health as you start to get older. I see your blood work looks good. Your cholesterol levels are good along with your prostate. Let's get started on the physical, and we'll have you out of here before you know it."

After the physical, Dr. Jones summarized things with Chris.

"You're in excellent health for your age. You take no medications and don't smoke or drink excessively. Here is my advice. The two things that can kill you in the next twenty years are prostate cancer or colon cancer. Stay on top of these with regular examinations, and you should be fine. Therefore, in addition to this physical, I recommend you have a colonoscopy to screen for colon cancer."

"Will this take much of my time? I have an important trip coming up soon," Chris asked.

"Not at all. You'll need to do the bowel prep the day before and take the day of the procedure. And you'll need a person to drive you back after the procedure due to the anesthetic you'll be given."

"OK, I'll set it up soon and get it over with," Chris replied.

"It's not as bad as people say it is. However, it's important to have it done as a preventative measure," Dr. Jones told Chris to ease his apprehension. "I'll have my office set up an appointment for you."

"Sounds good," Chris said as he shook hands with the doctor and left the exam room.

FIVE

Chris headed home to get ready to go out with Candace. He was a little hesitant about asking her to go with him for his colonoscopy. It made him feel like the other old guys his age and reminded him he was a lot older than Candace. After relaxing for a while and watching some news on a cable network station, he called Candace about picking her up.

"Hey there. I was just wondering if you're ready for me to pick you up?" Chris asked, expecting her to say to stop by as soon as he can.

"Hi. You know I've been so busy at work that I lost track of time. Let's just meet at the restaurant," she replied, half-listening to Chris as she was replying to an email.

"OK, I'll meet you in a half hour," Chris said, annoyed at hearing her typing in the background.

"So, how was your day?" Candace asked as she gave Chris a hug and a kiss at the entrance to the restaurant.

"Busy as usual. Let's get a table and glass of wine, and I'll tell you about it," he suggested, also thinking about telling her about his upcoming colonoscopy.

After being seated and ordering dinner, Chris began to share. "This morning, I had a meeting with an important client and had to lie a little bit to keep them happy," he said.

"No big deal. I'm sure this is business as usual," she reassured him. Everyone needs to stretch the truth occasionally. It's just the way it is." She responded quickly with a smile to negate any guilt he may feel about it.

"I guess you're right about that. Another thing I did was I had a physical today."

"Why did you need a physical? You aren't sick, are you?" Candace asked with a concerned look.

"No, I'm not sick. It's just because I turned fifty recently, as you may remember," Chris said with a smile remembering the big party she had for him.

"Why do you need a physical just because you turned fifty years old? You look fine to me, even for an older guy," she teased him.

"Thanks for reminding me I'm twice your age."

"We have had this discussion before. It's no big deal to me. I find you much more interesting to be around than guys my age. They are so immature."

"So, I am so mature," Chris replied, knowing their age difference didn't matter to her, but he was still not sure if it mattered to him. Although, he really enjoyed being with her, he usually didn't dwell on the age issue.

"Another part of turning fifty is having a screening colonoscopy. My doctor said I'm in good health, but I need to stay on top of having regular colonoscopies along with annual physicals that include prostate exams. I need to ask you a favor."

"Sure, whatever you need, I'm here for you," she said as she leaned toward him across the table.

"I'll be given a sedative before the colonoscopy, and I need to have someone drive me home after the procedure. Can you do this for me? You'll need to take a day off from work."

"No problem. We can go to lunch afterwards. I've been so busy; it will be a nice break. Although, I can't remember the last time I was in a hospital. I remember being in one to have tubes put in my ears when I was a kid. I had a lot of ear infections."

"Thanks! I'll let you know when I set up the appointment," Chris said with a bit of relief in his voice.

"By the way, this won't interfere with our upcoming plans to get away for a weekend?" Candace asked.

"No way. It takes one morning, and we are done. Life will go on as usual," Chris assured her.

"I don't want anything to change things between us," Candace said in a serious tone as she was looking directly into Chris' eyes.

"I promise you—nothing will change between us. We control our own destiny," Chris said, as he stared back into her eyes.

SIX

I *never really felt extremely comfortable in hospitals—all these sick people. People even die here!* Candace thought as she waited for the doctor who was performing a colonoscopy on Chris and looked around the waiting room. *I don't know how he talked me into this. I should have told him to get one of his friends to take him to the hospital and drive him home. Even the smells here are starting to get to me. I wonder what's taking so long.*

Maybe my friends are right. I shouldn't be dating a guy that is old enough to be my father! I don't care. Chris is fun to be with and much more mature than guys my age. I just can't handle them sometimes. However, I doubt any of my friends are in a hospital waiting for the results from a colonoscopy."

Candace was sitting in a waiting room with several other people nearby. The television had a cable morning news show running. She thought how she never watched the news and wondered how many people sitting there are interested.

Why do they always have the news on? she wondered, slightly annoyed. *The smells in here are starting to make me sick. I wonder how many diseases I can get by just sitting in here and breathing the air.*

As she was sitting, various doctors were paged over the

public address system. Occasionally, a doctor would come into the area to talk with someone who she assumed was a family member of the patient being discussed. Finally, Chris' doctor appeared in the hall and was walking towards her.

"Hi, Candace, I am Dr. Johnson. I want to give you the results of your father's colonoscopy."

"Wow! This is awkward. I am his girlfriend," she replied.

"Oh, I'm sorry. However, the consent form he signed authorized me to provide you with his medical information since he is still groggy from the anesthesia."

"OK, so how'd it go?"

"Well, I found only one polyp. But it was too large to remove during the colonoscopy without risking perforating the colon wall. I recommend he have it removed surgically as soon as possible. It appears to be benign, but I took some samples for a preliminary biopsy to verify. A complete biopsy of the polyp will be done after it is removed. Also, he will need about six weeks to recover at home. Here is a picture of it."

"Oh, my God! That looks so weird. It looks like a bunch of mushrooms inside a tube," she said with her eyes wide open.

"That is the polyp inside the wall of the colon." Dr. Johnson pointed to the picture with a pencil in a matter-of-fact voice. "Do you have any other questions?"

"What should I tell him? I never had to deal with this kind of stuff before," she said confused.

"Have him call my office and make an appointment to see me next week," Dr. Johnson replied calmly.

"Also, here are his discharge orders. Please sign at the bottom to acknowledge our discussion."

After he left, Candace sat in a chair in shock.

I thought this was a routine procedure. I never heard of anyone needing surgery to remove a polyp. This was supposed to be a one-day event. What am I going to say to Chris? she thought with a look of desperation on her face.

As she looked around, people were coming and going like everything was fine while her world had been turned upside down. She decided to just sit and wait for Chris to be brought out after the procedure. Almost an hour later, a nurse told her that Chris would be down soon, and she should get her car.

About ten minutes later, Christopher Baldwin was brought to the car in a wheelchair. Candace was driving Chris' luxury BMW SUV.

I cannot believe how much money he spent on this. Hopefully, there is some left over for that big engagement ring I have been waiting for, she thought as she pulled up to the entrance door to pick up Chris.

"So how did things go?" Christopher asked Candace as they left the hospital driveway for his house in the Los Angeles suburbs.

"You won't believe this. You got this huge thing called a polyp that the doctor could not get out, so you need to have surgery," she blurted out to him.

"What? Are you sure you heard him right?" Chris asked in disbelief.

"Yes, I'm sure. He also said you need up to six weeks for recovery at home."

"What? I'l be at home for six weeks? I can't stay away from work that long. I have important client meetings and a trip to Europe to close an important deal."

"Also, don't forget we were planning a weekend getaway to Vegas in a couple of weeks."

"I can't believe it. I just don't have time for this. Maybe I can put this off until it fits into my schedule."

"Dr. Johnson told me to tell you to make an appointment with him next week to discuss the surgery and biopsy results."

"What biopsy?"

"He thought it was OK, but he took samples for tests. Also, he'll need to evaluate the whole thing when it's out."

"This could be cancer?" Chris exclaimed in a loud voice.

"He didn't think so."

"Great. I don't have time for this. Just get me home so I can think things through," he said exasperated.

During the drive home Chris said nothing more. After leaving Los Angeles, they headed north on the 405 and then exited onto the I-5 heading for his home in Valencia. An hour later, they arrived.

Chris thought about how much he enjoyed the year-round warm weather that this part of California had to offer. He hated the winters in Chicago where he lived for many years prior to his divorce.

"We're here already. It feels like we just left the hospital," Chris said with a look of confusion.

"It's probably the anesthetic. The doctor said you may have some memory gaps for a while. Do you remember talking about you needing surgery?"

"Unfortunately, I remember that all too well! Just get me inside and leave me alone today. I need to think about things."

Candace sighed and helped Chris into the house as he was still unsteady. The front door opened into a spacious living room which was part of an open floor plan.

"Do you need anything? I can stay awhile," Candice offered, not sure what to say.

"No. I just want to be by myself," he replied sharply to her.

Candace left and Chris laid down on a large leather couch in the living room and dozed off for a while. He slept soundly for a couple of hours. He had not slept that well in a long time. He was always thinking about work, even when trying to sleep. Upon awakening, he called Dr. Johnson's office to make an appointment for the following week.

I don't know how to handle this. My absence for six weeks will throw everything in turmoil. It's hard for a business development vice president to take the weekend off, never mind six weeks! he thought with a deep sigh.

I should have never taken my doctor's advice about getting a so-called, "routine screening" colonoscopy at my last physical, just because I turned fifty recently. I know lots of guys that have had them and the most that ever happens is the doctor removes a couple of small polyps. I never heard of them being too big and needing surgery. I will just have to explain how busy I am to Dr. Johnson and how this must wait until I can fit it into my schedule later this year.

SEVEN

The next day, Chris drove to work. *What should I tell my boss? Everyone is counting on me to pull off this deal in Europe. I can't let them down. Never mind this may drop me from consideration for executive VP,* Chris thought in desperation. The traffic was worse than usual on the 405 going into downtown Los Angeles. He missed the train system in Chicago that he used to go into the Loop for work, although he had gotten used to driving to work each day.

As he approached the downtown area, the large buildings were starting to dominate the skyline. As he had done in Chicago, he worked in one of the taller buildings in the downtown area. Chris drove into the building parking garage and parked in a reserved space. He entered an elevator that would take him to the top floor of the office building to see his boss, the president of the company.

Chris entered the company president's large office with a magnificent view of downtown Los Angeles and sat down in a wing back chair. He felt like he was in someone's living room instead of an office. He briefly imagined himself in this office someday.

"So how did your colonoscopy go?" his boss asked.

"To tell you the truth, I'll need surgery to remove a polyp that was too large to remove during the procedure," he said as his back stiffened in the chair.

"Hopefully that can wait a while. I'm counting on you to close that deal in Europe in a few weeks. This has huge promotional implications for you too. As you know, there is the executive vice president position available for the right person. You bringing this deal home would put you on the top of the list."

"Yes, I understand. I have an appointment with my surgeon next week to discuss this. I plan to suggest we put this surgery off for several months. There is too much at stake here to let anything slow me down."

"That's the kind of attitude I saw in you when I decided to hire you. You always put the company first. You know, it's people like us that keep corporations moving forward and jobs secure for all their employees."

"After my divorce, this job looked extremely attractive. In addition to the professional opportunities, I felt I needed a change of scenery from Chicago, and LA looked like a great option. It has been great here, and I appreciate your confidence in my abilities."

"Well, just keep me posted on things." the president said as he stood and patted him on the back before Chris left the office.

He walked down the hall to the elevator. His office was a few floors below.

He settled into his office to catch up on missing a day at work. Although not as large as the president's office, he still had a pleasant view of the downtown area.

I can't believe how email piles up even when I am gone just one day! Christopher thought. *Let's see when those client meetings are coming up. In addition to the European trip, these meetings are also important. I brought them to the company, and I need to keep close tabs on them.*

"Hey there, partner, how are things going?" Sam, another vice president asked Christopher as he stuck his head into his office and interrupted his thoughts on the upcoming meetings.

"OK, I guess. Come on in and have a seat," Chris said nervously.

Sam found a wooden chair and pulled it in front of Chris' desk and sat down.

"How did your colonoscopy go yesterday?"

"Everyone seems to be interested in that subject lately!" Chris said with frustration. "As I told the president, I need surgery to remove a polyp that is too large to remove during the procedure."

"Wow! I bet you didn't see that coming."

"You can say that again. Worse yet, I'll need to take six weeks off from work."

"Hey, you can't even consider doing that right now. You have several big commitments coming up."

"I know."

"Besides, the rumor mill said you are on the short list for the executive vice president job. If you miss these meetings, who knows, someone else may slip into the slot."

"You really think so?"

"Sure. You know there are several people trying to one up you on this one. I am not included, of course."

"Of course not," Chris said sarcastically.

"Seriously, I'm not interested. I already have too much

travel and time away from the family. I sometimes wonder if I should not have been so career ladder focused…although the money is great."

"Are you serious? Doesn't your family enjoy all those extras they can afford with your income?"

"Yea, but I feel I miss a lot of little things like baseball games and school plays."

"That's what your wife is there for. You need to focus on supporting the family."

"Well, my wife may not agree with you on that one. I hope you can work everything out," Sam said as he left Christopher's office.

I can't believe what I just heard. Sam is not interested in this chance of a lifetime. I just don't understand his thinking about spending more time at home. I didn't spend a lot of time at home, and my kids are doing just fine, he thought as he stared out of his office window at the traffic jam on the 405.

The next week Chris headed out of his house for his appointment with Dr. Johnson. His doctor was in Valencia and so he set up an early morning appointment. He thought getting to work late would also avoid some of the daily traffic congestion he always dealt with.

He arrived at a medical office complex of buildings. It was like a maze finding his doctor's office. Chris stopped to recheck the building number and office number. He looked around the parking lot and finally figured out where his doctor's building could be found. He parked the car and entered the building. He then checked the building directory found just inside of the entrance door and soon entered a relatively small waiting room with a few people sitting in leather upholstered chairs and couches.

This is more comfortable than my office! Chris thought as he checked in with the front desk attendant.

He was on time and his name was called by a nurse a few minutes after he sat down and got comfortable. Instead of going into an exam room, Chris was escorted to a well-furnished office. He was told to make himself comfortable, and the doctor would see him shortly. A few minutes later, Dr. Johnson knocked on the door and entered the room.

"Hi, Mr. Baldwin, how are you feeling since the colonoscopy?" Dr. Johnson asked as he entered his office where Christopher was waiting. He was used to seeing doctors in exam rooms, but this looked more like his own office with pictures, certificates, and awards hanging on the wall. He also noticed family pictures on the desk and realized there were none on his own desk at work.

I bet he spends lots of time with his family, he thought, remembering his conversation with Sam.

"OK. I think. I'm back to my usual diet now."

"Great. Look, we need to discuss this large polyp. The good news is the biopsy reports show the samples I took are benign. Once it is completely removed, we will verify if it is a benign polyp, which I am confident it is. In addition to the biopsy results, you have no symptoms of cancer. However, I'm glad you came this year and not next year. One never knows for sure what these polyps will do."

"That's good news. Do you think the surgery can wait a few months? I'm in the middle of several important business matters that need my attention."

"I would recommend against that. I recommend the polyp be removed within the next few weeks. As I said, I do not want to leave this in your colon to possibly become cancerous."

"So, if I leave it for several months, things may go south on me?"

"That's one way to put it."

"Are you sure it can't wait? As I said I have several important matters to tend to."

"Look, you're an extremely fortunate man to have had this found now and not later. Your business life needs to wait so you can take care of this and recover from the surgery."

"So, what am I looking at?"

"Well, you'll be in the hospital for about three days and at home resting for six weeks. Also, you will be limited in lifting and exertion during that period so it would be best if you have someone around to help you out."

"OK, I guess we need to go ahead with the surgery as soon as possible. Well, my ex-wife and kids live in Chicago, but I'll see if my girlfriend, Candace, can help."

"Great! Please contact my office to arrange a surgery date."

"Thanks," Christopher said as he shook Dr. Johnson's hand as he left.

EIGHT

That evening as he was driving home, Chris thought about having Candace take care of him and wondered how that would work out. She was much younger than him and although they got along well, he was not so sure she was ready for this challenge. She seemed to just like having fun and being with him or her friends.

After arriving home, Chris went out to the mailbox to check his mail. Afterwards he sat down in the living room to watch the local news and began thinking about what he was going to say to Candace about his surgery. He still couldn't believe he would be out of work for up to six weeks. After dinner, he decided to call Candace.

"Hi, it's me. I need to discuss my visit to Dr. Johnson," Christopher began.

"So, how'd it go?"

"Well, as it turns out I need to have the surgery very soon, not later. Things look OK for now, but he does not feel comfortable waiting several months. He said I need to be at home recovering for about six weeks, and I'll need help. I guess I am asking you if you can do this."

"I don't know, Chris. You know this new job I have has

me traveling every week. The pay is good, and I don't want to risk being fired," she said with an apologetic voice.

"Will you just talk with your boss about it and see if you can take some time off from travelling?"

"Look, I really like this job and don't want to upset things just after starting it. I'm sorry, but I just can't help," she said more firmly.

"OK, OK. I'll just have to think about another alternative," he said with frustration in his voice as he finished the call with her.

That's just great. I guess I can't count on even those closest to me for help! I wonder how much worse this will be with my boss when I tell him I will be out for a few weeks, Christopher thought, feeling that all his plans were now collapsing, and he was not in control of his life any more.

Chris laid down on the couch and turned on the television to watch the Los Angeles Dodgers baseball game. He was a big Chicago Cubs fan and missed not seeing those games. He fell asleep watching the game and woke up around midnight and went to bed. He couldn't help worrying about what he was going to do about getting help after his surgery, so his night was a long one.

The next morning, as he headed for work, he was still thinking about where he would stay after his surgery and what would happen with his job while he was out. As usual, there was congestion on the 405 on his way to work. After getting into the office, he decided to talk with Sam.

"Hi, Sam. Can you stop in my office for a few minutes?" Christopher asked as he saw him in the hall.

"Sure. What's happening?"

"It looks like I need to have the surgery as soon as possible.

My doctor doesn't want to delay much, although he believes things are OK right now. So, I'll be out of work for six weeks. On top of that, I'll need help at home and my girlfriend, Candace, will be traveling and not available. What a mess!" he exclaimed, throwing his hands in the air.

"Have you told the boss yet?"

"No. That's my next stop."

"So, what's going to happen with the deal in Europe and your key client meetings here?"

"I don't know. Someone must take them over. This is such bad timing. Whoever takes over will probably receive the full credit for all the groundwork I did and get the promotion to executive vice president."

"That would be a tough break. As I said, there are several people who would jump on this opportunity."

"Yeah. I'm sure someone will capitalize on my misery!"

"So, what are you going to do about getting help? You could hire someone."

"I thought about that, but having a stranger in my house seems very weird to me."

"So, what other options do you have?"

"One that I don't know I can pull off. I'm going to call my ex–wife and see if I can stay with her and the kids in Chicago."

"Unbelievable! If I understand things right, you hardly ever have contacted her or your kids since the divorce and you moving to LA."

"I do try to call about once a month. You know how busy things get here."

"What do you think she'll say?"

"Probably no, and I then need to convince her it will work out."

"Good luck with that," Sam said as he left for a meeting.

Chris spent time staring out of his window at downtown Los Angeles, thinking about what he was going to say to the president about being out of work for several weeks. He was also wondering what would happen with his impending promotion while he was gone. After about thirty minutes went by, he decided to see the president.

"Hey, Susan, can I have a word with Don, if he isn't busy?" Christopher asked the president's administrative assistant.

Smiling at him, Susan nodded that now was a good time.

"Hi, Don. Thanks for making time for me to discuss something," Christopher said as he sat down in the same wingback chair he had sat in previously and still marveled at the view of downtown Los Angeles.

"What can I do for you?" Don asked.

"As a follow-up to our earlier discussion about my surgery, my doctor does not want to wait until later this year to perform it. So, it looks like I'll be out for six weeks," he said nervously.

"What about your trip and your key client meetings here?"

"Someone else will need to cover for me."

"There is no 'someone else!'" the president snapped back with a bit of frustration in his voice. "Our business is depending on you being successful with these clients."

"I'm sorry but at this point my health needs to be my top priority," he replied with a calm voice, trying to keep his composure.

"OK, I understand. I'll discuss possible people to cover for you."

"Thanks. Also, since I need help during my recovery, I may be in Chicago at my ex-wife's home with my kids."

"Maybe it will give you time to catch up with them."

"Yea, which may be a good use of my spare time. I'll keep in touch from Chicago."

"Good luck with your surgery," Don called out to him as Christopher left the office.

Well, that went as well as could be expected. Now the hard task is at hand—convincing Elizabeth to allow me to stay at her home, Christopher thought as he made the two-hour drive home from downtown LA, fighting traffic all the way.

NINE

Chris arrived home and sat down in his living room just staring at the wall. He was thinking about what to say to Elizabeth when he called. He was trying to imagine being back in Chicago for six weeks, living in his old house. That all seemed like ancient history. He was nervous about how his kids would receive him after all this time away.

I'm not sure what to say when I call. I guess I'll tell it like it is and see what happens. I really don't blame her if she pushed back on this idea. I have had so little contact with her and the kids since coming to LA, although I always make the child support payments on time. That may count for something. I must admit that I have felt free since the divorce.

Before I felt trapped with all kinds of responsibilities and re-lationship issues with Elizabeth. We just couldn't agree on anything, Chris thought after getting home and preparing to call Elizabeth.

Finally, he decided to make the call.

"Hello."

"Hi, Elizabeth, this is Chris."

"So, what is the honor you bestow calling me today?" she asked harshly.

"I deserve that and more. I know I have not been particularly good at keeping in touch," Chris said in a low voice.

"That's an understatement! I don't know if the kids would recognize your voice," Elizabeth said, raising her voice.

"Well, that may change soon," Chris replied calmly.

"What do you mean?"

"As part of turning fifty, I had a screening colonoscopy done recently. The doctor found one polyp that is too large to remove during the procedure, so it needs to be removed surgically. It appears to be benign, but he does not want to wait on it."

"So, what does that mean for me and the kids?" she asked, puzzled.

"I'll need someone to help me out with things while I'm recovering for six weeks. I have no one here to help, and I'm asking if I could have the surgery in Chicago and stay at your home while recovering?"

"What about your cute young girlfriend, Candy?" Elizabeth replied sarcastically and bitterly.

"That's Candace, and she'll be traveling for work and not be available," Chris said calmly, trying to not escalate the tension.

"So, you figure I'm available and will just say OK. Forget about how our marriage ended, that you have ignored the kids who really need a father in addition to a mother. You have no idea what they are going through, and what I must deal with. John is flunking several classes and had some suspensions. Next year he will be a senior. I have no idea if he will even qualify for junior college! Sarah has been hanging out with a questionable crowd since starting high school. Jennifer is still young enough. I think I still have some influence on her as a seventh grader. I can only hope for the best for her," she said, almost without pausing to take a breath.

"I didn't know how bad things were."

"You would if you bothered to be part of their lives. So, what do I tell the kids? Should I say Dad is stopping by for a few weeks because he has no better alternative? Besides, I don't have a spare bedroom for you."

"Look, I know I have not been a particularly good father, but I really need your help. Perhaps I can try to reconnect with the kids while I am there. You know I'm desperate when I'm asking you for this favor. I can stay on the couch. That will be fine."

"Well, maybe it would be good for the kids to see you for a few weeks, at least," Elizabeth said after an exceedingly long silence.

"Great! I'll contact my doctor to arrange for the surgery in Chicago. I'll let you know when things are scheduled."

"So, the polyp looks benign?" she asked with surprising concern.

"Yes, the preliminary biopsy came back normal. A full biopsy will be done after it is removed. However, the doctor is confident it should be fine, especially since I have no cancer related symptoms."

"Well, despite all our problems, I am glad to hear that. Let me know when you'll be arriving in Chicago."

"Will do and thanks very much, I know I'm asking a lot."

"No problem. We may be divorced, but we're still family."

The next day Chris decided to have dinner with Candace to tell her about his plans to go to Chicago for his surgery and stay at his ex-wife's home to recover.

"Hey there; how's your day going?" Chris asked Candace after she answered his call late in the morning.

"It's been crazy here. I have several trips planned in the next few weeks, and I need to get so much done here at the office. I'm not sure how I will get all this done!"

"Let's get together for dinner tonight. It sounds like you are having a rough day, and we can relax a bit."

"That sounds great. How about that Italian restaurant near your house for dinner around seven?"

"Sounds good to me," Chris replied. He was glad he'd decided to wait until dinner to discuss his plans for his recovery.

"Hi there," Chris said as he stood up from the table and kissed Candace when she arrived.

"I see you already ordered wine for both of us."

Chris thought this might make telling her he was going to stay with his ex-wife and his kids easier.

"I can't believe how busy this new job has gotten to be. I sometimes miss my old one. Of course, I miss not seeing you every day at the office," she said as she smiled and held his hand across the table.

"So why not come back? "I'm sure you'll be able to get your old job back," Chris said as he thought this might be an opportunity to have her available to take care of him after his surgery, although he knew that would not happen.

"Are you kidding? This new job offers me growth potential. I get to travel and get the 'big picture' view of the company and exposure to high level management. This is just what I've been looking for. I didn't spend four years at USC to end up in a dead-end job."

"Why do you call your old job a dead end? You had potential there too."

"Well, I could see moving up a couple of levels there. But to really move up to executive levels, like you are at, I needed new opportunities. Isn't that why you took this job in LA?"

"You're right. I was also looking for career advancement, and this job was a great step up the corporate ladder, although I do miss seeing you at the office every day," Chris said, realizing he and Candace were two of a kind. This somehow scared him a bit, and he wondered what their career aspirations meant for their personal relationship.

After ordering dinner, Chris decided to break the news about his plans to go to Chicago.

"I need to tell you about my plans for my upcoming surgery and recovery. As you talked about tonight, your travel schedule is heavy and doesn't let you be available to help while I recover. There are not many options for me here in LA. So, after a lot of thought, I decided to ask Elizabeth about staying at her house in Chicago while I recover."

"What! You are going to shack up with your ex-Liz!" Candace said, almost jumping up from her chair. She tried to keep her voice low so others around them wouldn't hear her.

"First, her name is Elizabeth, and secondly, I'm not shacking up with her. I just needed help and she agreed, although not until after some persuasion on my part. Do you have any better ideas?" Chris replied calmly.

"No, but this is not a good choice. She agreed to have you stay there, hoping she might get you back."

"No, that's not her reason. In fact, she said she's doing this because she thought we're still family."

"What does she mean by that?"

"I didn't ask her since I was happy just to have her agree. But now that you asked, I think she was referring to our three children. They're still my kids, regardless of my relationship with Elizabeth."

"There you go. She'll use your kids to get to you. She's probably jealous of your relationship with me and desperate for a relationship with a man in her life. You know, she is middle aged and tied to three kids at home."

"Hey, I'm about her age, and you don't say that about me."

"You're different. You don't act like you're fifty. You like to have a good time, and I might add, look a lot younger."

"Well thanks for the compliments," Chris replied with uncertainty as he wondered if that was a good reflection on him or not.

"Can't you do something else? I really don't like the thought of you spending six weeks at your ex's house. Also, won't the kids get in the way of you just relaxing and getting better? They will probably be bothering you to do all sorts of things like going to games or other school stuff that kids do. You told me they always were bothering you about going to events and taking you away from your priority, your job."

"Look, they're in school all day, and Elizabeth gets home a couple of hours after them. I'm sure I can handle things. Also, I can use my surgery as an excuse not to do anything with them. Even Elizabeth can't argue with me about that."

"Well, I don't know what to say. I really don't want you to go, but I also can't tell my boss that I will need to stay in LA to take care of my boyfriend. I'm sure that will not look good for my career growth. They need to know my job comes first."

"I understand. I hate to admit it, but I would probably do the same thing if I were you. However, that means we both must make tough choices. For me, that means staying with my ex and the kids for six weeks, while I recover. From what she told me, the kids are not doing very well in school or with their choice of friends. So, I'll probably have to deal with some stuff I really don't know what to do with."

"Don't sweat it too much. That's their mother's problem, not yours. You need to focus on your job and us in LA, not your ex and your kids in Chicago. They will be fine. I know lots of divorced people with kids, and they all do fine. Kids rebound easily, probably better than their parents," Candace replied dismissively.

"I hope you're right about that. Like I said, we all need to make hard choices at times."

"I'll just have to deal with you being in Chicago for the next six weeks. Promise me you'll call me every day. I probably shouldn't say this, but I really have strong feelings for you. We just seem to see the world the same way. Most people just want the American dream of getting married, buying a house, and having kids. We both want to leave our marks on the world. That doesn't happen with just being like everyone else just settling for the American dream.

"I never thought about it that way, but I think you're right. So, it's settled. Let's toast to six weeks changing nothing between us and getting back to where we left off today," Chris said as he and Candace each raised a glass of red wine.

TEN

The day before Chris called Elizabeth, she arrived at work a few minutes ahead of her 8 am meeting. Fortunately, her office was only a few miles from where she lived so she didn't have to deal with all the traffic when commuting into downtown Chicago.

The meeting was with upper management to discuss sales forecasts. She entered the conference room just in time for the meeting and saw that everyone was seated and waiting for her.

"I'm glad to see everyone is here. Sorry to keep you waiting," she told them, wondering why she was apologizing when she was there on time.

"As you can see, sales over the next few months may be down when compared to the past few months," she told the managers as she began her presentation.

"What's the cause for this decline?" one manager asked.

"I don't know. There are no obvious problems. I haven't had time to investigate the causes."

"You had better find the time. This decline could affect the company's stock value, and the shareholders will not be happy with that," another manager sharply replied.

"I will do so," she told him, trying to smile in the midst of her frustration.

Now where am I going to get the time for this? I can barely keep up with work and home as it is, she thought with frustration.

After the meeting, Elizabeth headed to her office to check her email.

Great! I missed a last-minute meeting with my boss because I didn't get here early enough to see his meeting notice. I think the company just figures I spend all my time and energy at work. No personal life! she thought as she got increasingly frustrated with her day.

"Hi, Samantha," Elizabeth said as she answered a call from her friend.

"Hi, Elizabeth. I was wondering if you are open for lunch today. We haven't gotten together for a while."

"Sure. I could use a break. The morning has not gone well."

"Let's meet at noon at our usual spot."

"That sounds good to me," Elizabeth said as she thought about her meeting and argument with her son John.

"So, how's your day going? Any better?" Samantha asked as she and Elizabeth sat down for lunch.

"About the same, as always, unfortunately. First thing this morning, I had my usual argument with John about getting out of bed and going to school. He said he was tired. This may be true since he hangs out with very questionable friends and comes home after one a.m.!"

"You let him stay out that late? Especially on a school night?" Samantha asked with astonishment in her voice.

"I used to fight him on this, but with work, the house, and the other two kids, I just don't have the energy left to argue with him. Or let alone stay up until he comes home."

"Look, I know it is hard being a single parent. I don't know how I would handle my kids without my husband's help. I may complain about him, but he does help when I really need it," Samantha said, sounding guilty of her own complaining about her husband.

"If Chris had stayed in the area after our divorce, he could at least have the kids' part of the week to give me some break. Instead, he decided to head off to LA. He claimed he left for career opportunities. I think he left so he could escape his own family. I know he always felt held back here in Chicago because of me and the kids not wanting to move elsewhere for his career."

"I know from my own experience that having moved for jobs can be incredibly stressful for the kids. They need to make new friends in new areas, which gets old fast," Samantha said, as she tried to be supportive of Elizabeth. "So, what's going on with John?"

"He has lost all interest in school. A lot of mornings he is either too tired or sick to go to school. I have tried counseling, but he will not cooperate. He doesn't take the sessions seriously. Before the divorce, he was a different kid. He is smart, but I am afraid he may just waste his life away if he doesn't get serious about school and his future."

"How are Sarah and Jennifer doing?"

"Sarah goes to school without any hassles, but she's taking extremely easy classes, starting to get too interested in boys, and hangs out with a sketchy group of girls at the high school. She was a different kid in junior high school. She took classes that challenged her, and she would talk about career goals.

"Jennifer is still doing well in school and is on a couple of sports teams. She's good friends with Jessica Chambers, one of our neighbor's kids. She has had a good influence on Jennifer. In fact, when Chris and I were married, our kids would play together with Michael and Jessica Chambers. We would even get together at weekends for barbecues.

"Those days seem so long ago. I hate to admit it, but sometimes I wish we could go back to those days. But that is not going to happen. So, I need to learn to move on with life. The kids also need to do so. It's impossible to go back to the way things used to be."

"You're right about that. What's going on with Chris? Have you heard from him lately?"

"He has a girlfriend. I guess his job wasn't such a high priority after all. Her name is Candy, and she is twenty-five! Can you believe that she is half his age? She could be his daughter. I also heard from the wife of one of his friends in Chicago that she's gorgeous. I'm not sure what she sees in Chris, especially his being much older. She's probably looking for an affluent older guy who won't mess around behind her," Elizabeth said, with a jealous tone. "Maybe that was part of the reason we got divorced—Chris wanted to be with someone younger. Never mind that we had three children together and married for twenty-plus years."

"Is her name really Candy?"

"No, it is Candace, but I prefer to call her Candy. It makes me feel better about her."

"You know, that's typical male behavior. They get divorced and start looking for an upgrade. Apparently, women in our age group aren't attractive enough for them. I think they're trying to relive their youth. Look, you're divorced; he's free to do what he wants and so are you," Samantha replied with an upbeat voice.

"Like I should go out on dates? I have no time to do my own job, never mind time for dating. At a meeting this morning I was told by one of the senior executives that I need to spend more time on my job. I thought to myself, that's easy for you to say. You probably don't need to get three kids out of the house every day and get home to get dinner started."

"I think your experience is typical for a lot of women. Even if they're married, they tend to do more of the work at home. You're doing fine. Don't let those guys get to you. I must get back to work. Let's do this again next week," Samantha suggested.

"Yea, let's do that. Sorry I complained so much today," Elizabeth told her as they were leaving the restaurant.

"No problem. That's what friends are for."

The day after Chris called Elizabeth, while they were eating dinner, Elizabeth decided to tell her children about their father coming to stay with them for several weeks.

"So, I need to discuss something with you that will affect all of us," Linda began nervously. She was not sure how her children would respond to their dad staying with them for six weeks while he recovered from surgery.

"Your dad called me yesterday about a medical exam he had recently. It is called a colonoscopy."

"What's a colonoscopy?" asked Jennifer.

"In a colonoscopy, a doctor sticks a tube with a camera up your butt," John interjects before Linda had time to respond. Although she didn't like her son John's interpretation, she did find it humorous and tried not to smile, let alone laugh aloud.

"Although crudely put, that's basically a reasonable description of the procedure. However, your brother neglected to point out the purpose for the colonoscopy. The doctor uses the camera to view the inner liner of the colon and look for any irregularities such as polyps."

"What are polyps?" Jennifer asked.

"Polyps are small growths that sometime occur inside the colon. They can look like small bumps. If they're present, the doctor can usually remove them during the procedure."

"Why do they want to remove them?" Jennifer continued with the questions.

"They can be precancerous or already a cancer, in some cases."

"So, what does this have to do with Dad and us?" Sarah asked, getting more interested in where this conversation was going.

"Your father has a very large polyp that couldn't be removed during the colonoscopy. So, he will have part of his colon removed that has the polyp during a surgical procedure."

"Is it cancerous?" Jennifer asked.

"The doctor did not think so. They'll know for sure once it is removed, and a lab can do a thorough biopsy on it."

"Now this is where you come into the picture. Your father will have this surgery in Chicago and will be staying with us for about six weeks to recover."

"Can't his cute girlfriend take care of him? It's not like we ever see him anymore," John yelled as he jumped up from his seat.

"Apparently, she'll be traveling on business and not available to help him," Linda said as she tried to keep a civil tone about Candace. She hated to admit to herself that she shared John's view about her. However, she tried not to talk badly about their father, although she knew at times, she did slip and said things that were not very favorable about Chris or his girlfriend.

"I know I have, at times, said some negative things about your father and his girlfriend, but he is still your father and therefore, he will always be part of this family, whether we like it or not."

"I don't know how you can support him, after all he has done. He left us to move to LA and shacks up with some girl half his age. Doesn't that get you angry?" John said to Elizabeth as he stared directly into her eyes.

"I admit his relationship with Candy does upset me at times," she said calmly in a low voice. "I am not sure why I agreed to let him stay here. I had considered this a perfect payback opportunity to say he couldn't stay here."

"Mom, I got to agree with John. I'm not sure I can handle him being here," Sarah told her and her siblings.

"Maybe things will change if he stays here for a while. You and dad may even get married again," Jennifer said wishfully.

"I'm afraid there's no chance of that happening, Jennifer. I know you really would like that, but there are things that no one can change," Linda said in a loving voice trying to suppress her own anger about Chris.

"Pastor Jim said that God can change anything," Jennifer replied.

"Honey, this is beyond hope, even for God," Linda said as she gave Jennifer a hug.

"There you go again with God fixing everything. If God cares so much about us, why did He let this all happen to us in the first place?" John said to Jennifer with an angry tone in his voice.

"I don't know, but I believe He does care about us all."

"John, that's enough! We all have had a difficult time dealing with the divorce and your father dating another person. I must deal with this all the time. For now, let it go and focus on the present situation," Linda told him in a calm voice.

"Where is he going to stay?" Sarah said she was trying to change the topic since she felt on the edge of losing her own composure if the conversation continued.

"He can use my bedroom," Jennifer offered.

"That's very thoughtful of you, but I told your father that he can sleep on a couch in the family room."

"That's where Toby sleeps," Jennifer protests.

"There are two couches. I'm sure your father and the greyhound can work it out," Linda replied, not wanting to make things too comfortable for Chris at her house.

"Look, I know none of us is happy with your dad's behavior, but as I told him, and I will tell you all here, we may be divorced, but we are still family. So, it is settled, and he will arrive in two days. I expect everyone to be on their best behavior and that includes me!"

Linda concluded the discussion, knowing she would be the most challenged to behave in a civil manner towards Chris.

However, she wasn't sure why she agreed to have him stay, but something had told her to agree.

"Hey, Mom. You letting Dad stay here is like the story of the Good Samaritan. He helped a man that was hurt when no one else would. Pastor Jim told us this story at the youth service," Jennifer told her mother.

"You know, I never thought about it that way," Elizabeth told Jennifer, trying to think about the parallel situation.

Later that evening, John, Sarah, and Jennifer discussed their father staying at their house while they were in the basement rec room watching a movie.

"This is going to be weird having Dad stay at the house. We haven't seen him since he went to LA a couple of years ago. I'm not sure what to even say to him. He doesn't even call much. I feel like I don't even know him very well," Sarah said, sadness in her voice.

"I don't see why his girlfriend can't take care of him. From what I hear Mom say occasionally, they're practically living together," John added defiantly.

"She told you that?" Sarah asked with surprise. She tried to avoid thinking of her father moving on.

"No, but I overheard her talking with a friend on the phone. She's still angry about things."

"She doesn't seem mad when she's around us," Jennifer said.

"That's because she doesn't want to upset us. Parents are like that. They think their kids don't see what's really going on," John replied. "A lot of my friends have divorced parents, and they tell me the same thing. Their parents don't talk much about how they really feel or ask their kids. They all pretend everyone is doing just great."

"Some of the kids with divorced parents at Lakeside Community Church tell me that they are having a lot of problems dealing with their parents' divorce but don't talk about it with them. They say their parents really try to ignore their problems," Jennifer added.

"Well, I'm doing just fine with my friends. We go out and party when we feel like it, and none of our parents bother us," John replied firmly.

"You know, John, I don't know if going out and getting drunk is a good way to deal with stuff," Sarah told him.

"It sure beats hanging around here all night. You notice

that Mom doesn't talk to us much. After dinner, she usually just watches TV or reads a book," he replied.

"Can we just change the topic; this is really starting to get to me. I just wish things could be the way they used to be," Jennifer yelled out as she tried not to start crying.

John and Sarah, seeing she was getting upset, stopped talking, and they all just continued to watch the movie in silence.

ELEVEN

Chris arrived at Chicago's O'Hare airport and headed for the luggage pickup area. He had packed a lot more than he was used to. Usually, he packed a duffle bag for a two- or three-day trip. This time he had two large bags with him.

After getting his bags, he headed for the van to take him to the car rentals. Even though he wouldn't be able to drive for a couple of weeks after his surgery, he wanted to be able to get around by himself as much as possible. He headed north on I-294 on his way to Evanston.

He drove into the old neighborhood with its mature trees and two-story brick homes. Professional landscape companies kept the lawns well-manicured. The trees lined the streets and supplied a canopy over the them. There were some young children playing in the front yard. They reminded him of when his children were young. *Life seemed so simple then,* he thought with a silent sigh.

The old neighborhood hasn't changed much. There are a lot more trees and greener lawns than in Valencia. The houses are different too. They're mostly four-bedroom colonials instead of the ranch style homes in California. The traffic here in Chicago was almost as bad as in LA, Chris thought as he drove towards the house he had lived in when he was married.

I'm a little afraid of how the kids will receive me. I haven't exactly been "father of the year" to them, even when I lived here. No one ever understood how important my job was for the whole family. They always demanded I be at all kinds of events like baseball games or concerts. I just couldn't take it anymore.

When Chris arrived at his family's home, he sat in the car and stared at the house. It was so much larger than his ranch style home in Los Angeles. This one was typical for the neighborhood, and the front yard had mature maple trees.

He finally decided to get out of the car. He went around and opened the trunk to get his two large suitcases and walked along a brick path to the front door.

Let's see how things go, Chris thought as he rang the doorbell with slight hesitation. He thought how strange it was to not just open the door and enter the house, like he did many years ago.

"Hi, Dad!" Jennifer yelled as she greeted him at the door and gave him a hug.

Chris was surprised and relieved at the warm greeting his youngest daughter gave him.

"I can't believe how you are growing. I guess it's been a while since I saw you last."

Toby the family greyhound also ran to him and jumped on him.

"I guess Toby is also happy to see me." Chris said, surprised at the dog greeting him. He almost forgot about the dog after being away so long. He somehow felt a little guilty about it.

"I really missed you, Dad," Jennifer said as they entered

the house. "Mom will be home soon from work. She told us about your surgery. Will you be OK?"

"I sure will be. But your dad needs to stay here a while to rest after his operation. Your mom said I can use the couch in the family room to sleep."

"I offered my room, but Mom said the couch would be fine for you."

"Like she said, I'm fine with the couch."

"Toby likes the other couch to sleep on so you two will be like roommates."

"I guess I can bunk with the dog too. Do you know where I can keep my clothes? There doesn't appear to be a closet or dresser in the family room."

"Mom said you can use part of the closet in her bedroom."

"That sounds good. So, how is school going?"

"Good. I have all A's and B's in my classes. I'm also on the girls' Lacrosse team."

"Wow. You must be a pretty good player."

"I'm OK. The coach said I have a lot of potential and should practice as much as I can."

"Well, even great athletes need to practice a lot to stay great."

"Where are John and Sarah?"

"They never get home right after school, but Mom insists they be home by dinner. She said it's important for us to have dinner together, but they don't always show up."

"What are they doing after school?"

"I don't know. They just hang out with friends."

"OK. I'll see you at dinner," Jennifer said with a big smile as she headed for her bedroom.

"Hey Jennifer, I'm home." Elizabeth yelled as she entered

the kitchen from the garage with some groceries in hand.

"Hi, Elizabeth," Chris said quietly as she entered the kitchen. He was drinking a glass of water.

"Oh, hey. I forgot to check when you would be getting here," she said with a distant sounding voice.

"Hi, Mom," Jennifer said. "It's going to be great having Dad here for a while!"

"Yes, it will be. Can you let Dad and I talk some before dinner?"

"Sure. I got to do some homework anyways."

"How was your flight?" she asked Chris.

"OK. Even in first class, it's a long trip. Again, I really appreciate you letting me stay here. Jennifer told me I'll be bunking with Toby."

"As you know there are no other bedrooms available. You certainly are not going to stay with me. Besides, you always liked Toby. He'll like the company," she said tersely.

"Well, I will take whatever I can get for space," he replied.

"This divorce has been very hard on the kids. I think John and Sarah were most affected. As I told you. they're hanging out with questionable friends, to say the least. I sometimes forget why we got divorced. It seems so long ago and in some ways, our old problems don't look that great now."

"Oh, come on. We could never agree on anything," Chris reminded her. "Your job always conflicted with mine. We could not agree on how to deal with kids, especially how to discipline them. Just to name a couple highlights."

"Do you mean we couldn't, or you wouldn't ever compromise on anything?" Elizabeth quickly replied.

"You mean you would not compromise on anything."

"Whatever. I guess at this point who cares, the damage is

done, we're divorced, and our kids are a mess," she replied with a surrendered tone in her voice.

"There's still time to turn things around," Chris replied quietly.

"You think so? John is a junior; he only has one more year before who knows what he will do after high school. And even Sarah has only a few years left. Our best hope is with Jennifer if I can ever figure things out."

"Maybe I can help while I'm here for a few weeks. I'll try to spend some quality time with each of the kids."

"It's not quality time they need from you. They need lots of time from you and maybe, if you are lucky, a little quality time will result. Besides, you think being here for six weeks will fix everything and then you can go back to your barely legal age girlfriend, Candy, and forget about us up here in Chicago."

"It's Candace, and she's 25 years old. And I do have to get back to earn a living to support two households."

"You could have kept your job here in Chicago. Why did you need to go to LA?"

"There were some great opportunities, and frankly I felt I needed a change of scenery after the divorce."

"Didn't you care that you would not see you children very often?"

"I figured we could keep in touch with calls and e-mail."

"Being a father is not a virtual activity like social media. It requires face time, and I don't mean on a cell phone!"

"Look, can we discuss this at another time? I just got in, and I need to get ready for my surgery in two days. I was lucky my surgeon knew someone in Chicago that he highly recommended. I told my boss about my plans to have it done in

Chicago. He was hoping to keep me nearer to the office for any questions that may come up while I'm on sick leave. I guess we can handle that with phones and e-mail. Did you plan in your work schedule for my surgery?"

"Yes, I did. I'll drop you off at the hospital in the morning and stop by after work to see you after your surgery. I should be there around the time it wraps up. I told the kids to order a pizza because I will be home late."

"I know we have a lot of unresolved issues, but I really do appreciate you taking me in for this surgery and recovery. Frankly, I don't know what else I would have done," Chris said with quiet sincerity.

"As I told you before, we may be divorced, but we will always be family with the kids. OK, enough of this. I'll get dinner ready and hopefully everyone will be there. Let's try to have you catch up on things with the kids."

"Sounds like a plan." Christopher said as he left the kitchen.

TWELVE

After a few more minutes of daydreaming, Chris decided he needed to get outside for a breath of fresh air. He walked into the backyard that had several tall trees in it. He remembered when they were much smaller when his family first moved into the house. The yard was fenced in so Toby could run around without a leash. The dog followed Chris outside and wanted him to kick a large red ball because he likes to catch it in the air. When Chris kicked the ball, the dog would run around for a while before bringing it to Chris and dropping it. He would then sit on the ground ready to run after the ball when Chris kicked it again. Chris was playing with the dog when a next-door neighbor saw him.

"Hey, Chris," Christopher's neighbor Paul Chambers yelled as he saw him in the backyard.

"Oh, hi there Paul. As they say, 'long time no see,'" Chris said as he walked over to the chain link fence.

"I can't remember the last time I saw you. Sorry to hear about your upcoming surgery."

"Bad news travels fast."

"My daughter Jessica told me. She and your daughter Jennifer are in the youth group at my church."

"I didn't know she was in a youth group at your church," Chris said with surprise.

"Yea, well, Jessica invited her to check it out last year, and she found she liked it. She has made several friends there."

"That's great. As you know, our family has never been churchgoers, except for Christmas and some Easters."

"No problem. Linda and I would be happy to have you and your family join ours sometime for a worship service while you're in the area."

"Thanks, but I'm not sure we're that comfortable with churches."

"So, how are things going for you in LA?"

"Great. Until this surgery thing came up, work has been going well. I've been in line for the executive vice-president position. Now being away, someone else is taking over some of my important accounts and will be closing an important deal in Europe in place of me. I'm not sure where this will leave me for the promotion."

"You know, I've been there. We moved here to Chicago from Seattle so I could take a high-level management job at Boeing headquarters. I thought that was what I wanted, but eventually I realized that I hated all the travel and being away from the family, especially my son. Michael was growing up and in high school, and I was missing a lot. As you know, I decided to leave Boeing to start an engineering consulting firm here. I don't travel nearly that much now and get to set my own schedule. I even teach part-time at Northwestern, which I could never have done before with my work schedule."

"I'm glad that worked out for you, but I still enjoy working up the corporate ladder. I like the challenges presented. That's partly why I left Chicago to go to the company in LA."

"So, what's the other reason?"

"Frankly, after the divorce, I needed to get away. Just too much stuff here."

"I've known you and your family for many years as neighbors. Our kids have been growing up together. So, I need to tell you, the kids have taken the divorce very hard. Jennifer shares some of her problems with Jessica."

"I know. Elizabeth has been telling me about it too. She said they need me nearby, but I just can't handle things here. I needed a change of scenery if you know what I mean."

"I hear you on that, but I have found that sometimes I need to just face things head on."

"Well, I tried that and found I couldn't handle things very well. Hey, I think dinner is about ready, so I need to go," Chris said abruptly, starting to feel very uncomfortable about facing perhaps a reality about himself. "It was great seeing you again. Say hi to Linda for me."

"Will do. I'll keep you and your family in my prayers. Good luck with the surgery."

"Thanks." Christopher said as he headed for the back door.

THIRTEEN

Chris entered the house through the back screened porch to the kitchen. As he entered the kitchen, he smelled food that he hadn't smelled in a long while. He had gotten used to eating takeout food or eating at a restaurant with Candace.

The children started to enter the kitchen one at a time and sat down at the table waiting for everyone to show up. Finally, when they all were gathered, Jennifer offered to say a prayer giving thanks before eating. After they glanced at each other with a surprised look, she went ahead. Chris couldn't recall a time when they had said a prayer before dinner, even at Thanksgiving.

"It's nice to see everyone again," Christopher said with a forced smile to John and Sarah with a bit of awkwardness in his voice as he sat down for dinner with his family for the first time since the divorce.

No one responded.

"So how is school going? I can't believe you two are both in high school now."

"OK, I guess," Sarah began, breaking the silence. "It's a lot different from Junior High School."

"How's your year going, John?"

"Like Sarah said, OK."

"Have you been thinking about colleges to apply to? You're in your junior year, and it won't be long before deadlines will be approaching."

"Not really. My grades really suck. So, I don't know what schools would be interested in me."

"Your mom told me you have been having problems with classes. Would tutoring help?"

"You know Dad, I'm not really very interested in school, getting good grades, and going to college."

"So, what do you want to do?" Christopher asked tersely, as he tried to keep his temper.

"I don't know. Most of my friends don't have any plans after high school. I figure I'll just see what happens."

"What do you mean, you'll see what happens? Being successful just doesn't happen. You need to be intentional and have a plan! I'll give you a clue—your friends will end up doing nothing and be living with their parents when they're 30 years old, if they're lucky," Christopher yelled at John after he lost all patience.

"What do you care? You're never around!" John yelled back as he jumped up from his chair and hurried from the room.

"Chris, try to keep your cool. You just got back here. Go easy on him," Elizabeth said in a very quiet voice.

"You're right. It's just that he has every advantage, and I hate to see him throw his life away doing nothing."

"So, Sarah, how are things with you?" Christopher said, trying to move on in a quieter fashion.

"My classes are OK; some more interesting than others."

"Have you thought about what careers might interest you?"

"A little bit. I've been thinking about business maybe."

"Have you made many new friends in high school?"

"Yea, a few. They seem to be more interested in dating and hanging out with older guys than with going out with me to shop at the mall or to movies."

"I think they're a little young to be dating."

"A lot of kids are dating in my grade. It's no big deal."

Maybe you should find friends not so interested in dating, Christopher thought with frustration. He decided not to say anything more to keep the peace, after he saw what happened with John. He turned his attention to Jennifer.

"Hey, Jennifer, I was talking with our neighbor Paul Chambers this afternoon. He said you've been going to the youth group at his church with his daughter Jessica."

"Yea, I've been going for a while. Jessica invited me last year. I know we don't go to church very much so I wasn't sure I would like it. But after going a few times, I met several kids like me, and I look forward to it now."

"What do you do there?"

"On a typical night, we play some games and do Bible studies. We also have a worship service just for teenagers. Pastor Jim, our youth pastor, is nice and told us how the Bible can be applied to what we experience in school or at home."

"I didn't know how much you've gotten into church."

"I've been thinking about getting baptized. Mom told me we were never baptized, and since I have committed my life to Jesus, Pastor Jim said that is the next step."

"What do you mean you committed your life to Jesus?" Chris asked skeptically.

"Just that; I have accepted Jesus as my Lord and Savior, and I'm trying to live the kind of life Jesus wants me to," Jennifer said as a matter of fact.

"Wow! I had no idea what you've been up to; I guess I need to talk with you more."

"That's what Mom said too," Jennifer quickly replied.

"I see. Well, I admit I've not been a very good dad. I'll try to make up some for it while I'm here." Christopher said with a bit of confusion in his mind. He was not sure what to make of Jennifer's sudden interest in church and Jesus.

"So, what's with Jennifer? What got her interested in church suddenly?" Christopher asked Elizabeth as he helped clean up the kitchen and dining room.

"I don't see anything wrong with it. At least she has a good group of friends. As you can see, the older two hang with a questionable crowd."

"Have you gone to Paul's church services?"

"No, although he and Linda have invited me and the kids. I just drop off Jennifer for the youth services or the Chamber's family brings her."

"Over the years, I guess we never saw much use for organized religion," Christopher said. "I remember going to church regularly as a kid, and I lost interest as a teenager."

"Me too. After we got married in my parents' church, we kind of lost touch with going," Elizabeth replied.

"What about John? What's your game plan?"

"What do you mean what's my game plan? You are his father. What do you think we should do?" Elizabeth quickly said in a sharp subdued voice.

"Well, you live with him and see him regularly. I'm not sure what to say to him."

"Whose fault is that?" Elizabeth asked defiantly

"Look let's not go over the same stuff again. You know the

job in Los Angeles will also help the kids here with my making more money."

"It's time, not money, that is sometimes really needed. Well, see what you can do while you're here."

"You know that I worked very hard for where I am today. I come from a working-class family, and my parents wanted their kids to do better than they did. I guess that's what I want for our kids. Maybe we made life here too easy for them, and they don't think they need to work for anything. I'll try to reach out to John while I'm here. I only want what's best for him."

They finished cleaning up, and Elizabeth headed for her bedroom and Christopher for the family room.

The next evening, Chris drank his first of two rounds of two pints of a liquid to clear his intestinal tract. He spent time after each round in the bathroom. After finally completing the second dose around midnight and feeling like he didn't have to go to the bathroom anymore, he decided to try to get some sleep.

Chris arranged his pillow and blanket as he lay down to watch the late news. Toby jumped up on the small adjacent couch that was perpendicular to his couch.

"I guess we better get used to spending a lot of time together the next few weeks," he said to Toby. "I'm not sure what to make of Jennifer getting so excited about God and Jesus," as he continued his monologue with the dog.

"I remember as a kid going to church. It seemed like that's just what everyone did. I didn't think much about it. I remember Sunday school classes and reading from small paperback booklets about characters from the Bible like Moses and David. Also, all those stories Jesus told people. What were they called? Oh yea, parables. I never quite got my head around all of them. My mother used to teach some of those classes. It seemed like only the moms' taught classes.

"I especially remember the Christmas programs. We did the same thing every year, reenacting the story of Joseph and Mary finding no room at the inn, and Jesus being born in a manger. We sang the usual Christmas carols. Even though we did the same thing every year, I think we all had a good time. The parents just liked seeing their kids in the program. I guess Christmas was my favorite time of year, especially the part about getting presents. As I got older, as a teenager, I also got to like Easter, but for the wrong reasons as I look back on things. I liked seeing all the girls dressed up for the holiday. I'm not sure I understood the real meaning of Easter. I remember hearing that Jesus died for our sins, but I still don't really get what that's all about.

"We never talked much about Jesus or God at home. I don't think anyone read the Bible. We didn't even say a prayer before dinner. It seems like church was just for Sunday mornings. The rest of the week, no one thought much about it.

"Once I got to college, I never even went to church on Sundays. I remember some students going to church and even asking others to come along. I thought they were kind of weird and just ignored them, like most other students did. Besides, after partying early into Sunday morning, who could get up to go to church?"

Toby decided to roll over on his back and lean against the back of the couch with his legs straight in the air. He groaned as he stretched to get comfortable.

"I remember my parents and Elizabeth talking about a church wedding after we announced our engagement. At the time, it seemed like a reasonable thing to do, but now as I think about it, it was more of a social obligation than anything else. After we got married, we rarely went to church except for Christmas and Easter. After moving for jobs a few times, we never settled in a church. The kids weren't even baptized. Our parents pushed us on that, and we kept saying we would get around to it, but over time, it never happened. I'm curious about Jennifer's interest in church. Well, at least it keeps her out of trouble."

Chris got very tired and went to sleep with the television still on. He woke up during the night and turned it off.

FOURTEEN

The next morning Chris and Elizabeth headed out for the hospital. Chris had said goodbye to the kids, and they wished him well with his surgery. Only Jennifer offered him a hug as she left. John and Sara just waved towards him when they went out the door.

Chris got into the minivan, and Elizabeth drove. He forgot what it was like in the minivan after driving his SUV around Los Angeles. He felt so domesticated and uncomfortable riding in it. They were driving to a large suburban hospital associated with the University of Chicago Medical Center. Chris was glad he didn't have to drive into the city for his surgery. They finally arrived at the entrance of the hospital.

"So here we are. I'll stop in after work to see how you're doing. I think you should be getting out of surgery by the time I'm back. I gave your surgeon's office my cell number, just in case I need to get back early," Elizabeth said jokingly.

"Thanks for the vote of confidence."

"Hey, I'm just kidding. You'll be fine."

"Thanks for getting me over here, and I'll see you tonight," Chris said as he headed out of the car with his duffle bag holding a few items for his hospital stay.

Chris walked into the lobby, looking for the registration desk when his cell phone rang.

"Hi, honey. How are you doing? This is your big day," Candace said in a chipper voice as Christopher answered his cell phone in the hospital lobby.

"I'm doing OK. I guess I'm a little nervous about the surgery," he replied hesitantly.

"Is anyone there with you?"

"No. Elizabeth dropped me off on her way to work and will be back tonight to check in on me."

"Wow! She couldn't stay for the day."

"Well, we are divorced, and she views this whole thing as doing me a favor." He told her as he thought sarcastically, *Why aren't you here, if we have such a great relationship with me?*

"I'm at the airport and need to board a flight soon. I'll call tonight to see how you're doing. Love you!"

"Have a good trip," Christopher said and tried not to sound annoyed with her as he ended the call.

Chris continued to look for the hospital registration desk. He spoke with the person there who took some information about him. He had been there the day before and supplied most of the information they needed, including his insurance. He also had a physical and blood work done the day before. The receptionist told him to have a seat, and a nurse would get him soon.

"Hi, Mr. Baldwin, we're ready to get you prepped for surgery," a nurse said as she escorted him into the surgical ward. He was seated in a wheelchair and was brought behind several closed doors marked "Authorized Personnel Only." It seemed to Chris like a maze of turns they made, and he had no sense of where he was in the hospital. Finally, they arrived at the room where he would get ready for the surgery.

He was told to take off all his street clothes and put on a gown that's difficult to close in the back. Chris thought about his butt hanging out of the gown as he walked around the room. He was told to lie down on a small bed, and the nurse inserted an IV needle into his hand. She was going to use his arm but could not find a vein. She said he may be dehydrated from the bowel prep he did the night before because it tended to dehydrate people and make it difficult to find a vein.

"Do you want me to call your family to come in and see you before your surgery?" the nurse asked, after he was in his hospital gown and an IV was set up.

"That won't be necessary. No one is here right now, but my ex-wife will be here when I get out of surgery."

"Do you want me to stay here while you wait?" she asked with a smile, feeling a little sorry for him but trying to not show it by framing her question in a non-emotional, professional sounding voice.

"No, thanks. I could use a little quiet time to collect my thoughts. This whole thing is hard to get my head around!"

"I know what you mean. Surgery is always a bit unnerving to folks. Well, if you need anything just push the call button by your side."

"Thanks."

FIFTEEN

A little while later, there was a knock at the door.

"Come on in," Christopher yelled, thinking it was the nurse checking up on him.

"Hi, I'm Pastor Jim Stone from Lakeside Community Church."

"I don't think I asked for a pastor to stop in before my surgery."

"You didn't. Your daughter Jennifer asked me to stop by. I am the youth pastor at Lakeside, and she attends the youth services and programs with Jessica Chambers. I believe she's your neighbor."

"Sure. Why did she ask you to stop by?"

"Well, she wanted to be here herself, but her mom said it was a school day, and she did not have time to drop her off at school after seeing you. How are you doing? I remember being nervous before my surgery a few years ago to have my appendix removed."

"I'm doing OK. So, are you going to pray with me before my surgery?"

"We can if you wish. I don't want to add more drama to this event, if you aren't comfortable with me praying."

"So, what do you want to do?"

"I just stopped by at the request of your daughter. She's concerned for you and wanted to make sure you weren't here all alone."

"Wow, I didn't know she cared that much. As you probably know, I haven't been around much since I divorced their mother."

"Well, I hear you will be around for about six weeks recovering before going back to Los Angeles. Maybe you can reconnect with them a bit while you're here."

"I've heard that before. How much can I do in six weeks?"

"Now that's an awesome question. You know six weeks is forty-two days. That's a little more than forty days. God can do a lot in forty days, let alone forty-two days!"

"Why do you think God can accomplish a lot in forty days?"

"Well, Moses spent forty days on a mountain and came down with the Ten Commandments written by God. Elijah, the prophet travelled forty days to reach the mountain of God and receive God's will for him. And Jesus spent forty days in the desert being tempted by Satan, and after the forty days of rejecting Satan, Satan left him, and He was attended by angels You see, forty days can have life-changing effects on people."

"So, you're saying a miracle with my relationship with my kids could happen while I'm here for just six weeks?"

"I think God is capable of changing much more than just that in your life in forty days."

"I don't attend church and don't believe in miracles, especially in my own life. Look what a mess it's in. I'm divorced, my kids hardly talk with me, and they're having their own problems! Why should I even believe there is a God? His presence isn't very evident in my life."

"God has worked through believers and non-believers throughout scriptures to carry out His will," Pastor Jim began. "I disagree with you about God not being present in your life. He is certainly present in your daughter's life, and that's why I'm here."

"So, you're saying that God may be reaching me through my daughter?"

"Exactly, so would you like me to say a prayer before I leave?" Pastor Jim asked confidently.

"Sure. I guess I can use whatever help I can get," Christopher replied with some confusion in his voice about their conversation.

"Lord, please be with Christopher and his doctors and nurses as they attend to him during and after his surgery. You are the Great Physician that can heal everything. Also, please use the time Christopher has here with his family to heal him physically and heal his relationships with his family. In Jesus' name, we pray. Amen."

"Good luck with your surgery. I'll stop by to see how you're doing tomorrow, if that's all right with you."

"Sure. Thanks for the prayers."

SIXTEEN

Your doctor has ordered you to have an epidural with a nerve blocker prior to surgery," the nurse said as she entered the room. "The nerve blocker will reduce the post-operative pain. Also, he wants you to take this stool softener with this little bit of water to help ease your digestion after the surgery."

After he took the pill, Chris laid down in his bed, and the nurse pushed him to another room where another nurse greeted them at the pre-op area.

"Just sit up on the side of your bed and put your face into this support."

"What's this for?" Chris asked.

"I'll give you a sedative to put you out for a couple of minutes while the doctor inserts the nerve block into your spine. It will numb the lower part of your body so when you wake up, you will not be able to move your legs."

"This sounds like what my ex-wife had before she had a C-section with one of our kids' birth. I don't remember her being given a sedative. The doctor just had her lie on her side and told her not to move while he inserted a large needle into her spine."

"This is similar, except since you're not pregnant, we can give you a sedative. We wouldn't want to sedate the baby for a C-section," the nurse told him.

"That's so weird, not being able to move my legs," Chris remarked after waking up and not remembering even going to sleep.

"Now you're ready for surgery," the doctor told him as the nurse pushed his bed to the operating room.

Wow, this operating room looks huge, Chris thought as they moved him from his bed to the small table in the middle of the room with several large lights overhead. He met his surgeon briefly.

"So, how are you doing?" the surgeon asked Chris.

"As well as I think I can be considering you are about to remove my appendix and about a foot of my colon."

"That's correct. We will be removing your ascending colon, appendix, and associated lymph nodes. As we discussed, I don't think there is any cancer present, but we will treat this as if it were cancer and make sure a large margin is taken. No worries, I do this all the time. You'll be fine," the doctor reassured Chris.

"OK, just breathe normally, and you'll go to sleep very quickly. When you awake, you'll be in your hospital room with all this over with," the anesthesiologist told him as he placed a small mask over Chris' face.

SEVENTEEN

That morning, Elizabeth had a major meeting with upper management to review the company's past quarter sales performance. She had gotten her bachelor's degree in marketing from Harvard but did not work outside of the home until Jennifer was in grade school. As she was driving, she was thinking about how she had decided to go back to work. If she hadn't, she was not sure how she would have supported herself and the kids after the divorce. Although she received child support from Chris, her own job made life a lot easier financially.

I guess that's another good reason to work outside of the home. You never know when your marriage will break up. I got to admit, even though Chris and I had problems, looking back, I'm surprised we got divorced, she thought as she arrived at the suburban office. She was glad she didn't have to go into the city every day as many of her neighbors did for work.

After the meeting, she had a message from Samantha asking if she was available for lunch. After an exceedingly long morning, she thought a long lunch hour might be in order. They met at their favorite restaurant, and after ordering lunch, they talked about their morning.

"How's your day going?" Samantha asked, as she thought about Chris having surgery that day.

"This morning's meeting was terrible. Everyone expects double digit improvements in sales every quarter! I gave them a reality check that did not go over well. However, they won't hassle me because they know I'm right."

"How's Chris doing?" Samantha asked directly, surprised that Elizabeth hadn't mentioned him.

"I guess he's fine. I dropped him off this morning, and I haven't heard from his doctor yet. He said he would call when the surgery was completed."

"Are you doing okay not being at the hospital?"

"Sure. I figured it would be worse just sitting around there waiting. His doctor said it could be up to a four-hour procedure not counting getting him prepped ahead of the surgery."

"That's a long day. I had my appendix removed a few years ago, and I think the whole thing took less than one hour."

"His doctor said that colon surgery is very time consuming. I'm amazed he'll do it with a laparoscope. The main incision will only be about three inches long," she explained.

"Are you concerned about him? You sound kind of clinical about it, even if he is your ex."

"OK, I guess I am concerned and not sure how I would handle waiting at the hospital. Being at work keeps my mind occupied on other things," she said with frustration about her mixed feelings.

"I'm sure he'll be fine. Here comes lunch, let me tell you about my morning," Samantha said, deciding it was a good time to change the subject.

EIGHTEEN

Hello there. How are you doing?" Elizabeth asked Christopher softly as he was still a bit groggy from his surgery that day.

"Hi. I guess OK. I'm still alive! I'm also not sore at all. It must be that the nerve blocker they gave me before surgery is still working," Chris said, still a little groggy.

He noticed an IV line in his arm. Also, he felt small pulses on his lower legs from a compression device used to prevent blood clots from forming in his legs until he started walking again. This reminded him he now had feeling back in his legs, but he had no pain. He thought about the nerve block still working. Finally, he noticed he had a catheter with a line taped to his left leg leading to a bag. He forgot about his doctor talking about that at his pre-op visit. Also, he wondered how he got into a different hospital gown than the one he wore going into the surgery.

"You're here early. I thought you would be here after work."

"Well, I checked with the hospital and heard you would be out a bit ahead of schedule. So, I thought someone should be here when you got to your room," she said with a smile.

"I appreciate that. I know you have a busy schedule at work," he said smiling back at her.

"I admit I was considering just keeping to my schedule. I had to move a couple of meetings. At the end of the day, I decided some things are more important than work."

"Elizabeth, I wish we could have agreed on that when we were married. We both put a lot of priority on our careers. I guess we still do."

"Yea, which has always been an issue. Do you remember how it was when we were dating in college? It seemed so simple. We'd each have successful careers, make lots of money, and have a great family. We'd even go on vacations all over the world."

"Sounds like a Norman Rockwell family. As we know, that was not reality. By the way, Pastor Jim Stone dropped by before my surgery. He said Jennifer asked him to visit. What do you make of all this church stuff she's getting into?" Chris asked with bewilderment.

"I don't really know. I never got into church much since getting confirmed as a teenager."

"Me neither. Church and the Bible just never seemed relevant to me. I'm not sure I even believe there is a God. Pastor Jim was telling me that my six weeks at home are like how God used forty days with several biblical characters spending time in the desert, on a mountain, or traveling to change their hearts to do His will. He suggested God may do something similar for me during my recovery."

"That sounds absurd!" Elizabeth said with a laugh. "Well, being a pastor, he probably must at least try to sell that thinking. Look how much time we spent in marriage counseling. A lot more than forty days and a lot more money! Since the divorce, I have had our kids in counseling, and you can see how that has gone with the two older ones."

"I don't think God really cares about what happens in our day to day lives, if there is a God at all," Christopher added quietly.

"Well, be careful what you say with Jennifer, she has really gotten into this. As you know, she even accepted Jesus as her Lord and Savior. She is now talking about being baptized since she wasn't before."

"What do John and Sarah think about all this?"

"Not much. Paul's son Michael has invited them to check out the youth group, but they aren't interested. They tell me only the weird kids go to church youth groups."

"I'm not sure about church and God, but I do know Paul's kids seem to be doing well. More than I can say about our two older ones."

"How's my patient doing?" Chris' surgeon said as he knocked on the open door and thought he might be interrupting a private conversation between Chris and Elizabeth. "I'm on my way home and wanted to check in on you."

"I'm doing well with no pain, which has surprised me."

"It's the nerve block we gave you prior to surgery. It will be effective for a while more."

"I can feel my legs now though."

"That part of the anesthetic wears off after a few hours."

"This is Elizabeth," Chris said, not sure how to introduce her. Saying she was his ex-wife sounded awkward.

"Nice to meet you. Chris told me he'll be staying with you and your children for the next few weeks."

"Yes, that's right. By the way, are there any updates on the polyp you removed?"

Chris was thinking the same question and was surprised that Elizabeth asked about it.

"My resident and I cut open the colon after removing the section and got a good look at it. It appears benign along with the lymph nodes that were removed. It was all sent out to a lab for examination, and we'll have the results next week."

"It sounds like we're going in the right direction," Chris added with a little bit of relief in his voice.

"I'll check in on you in the morning, so try to get some rest," the doctor said as he left the room.

Chris' phone rang. "I should get this," he said as he saw Candace was calling.

"That's fine. I need to get home and check in on the kids," Elizabeth said as she too saw the call was from Candace. She tried to pretend she did not know who it was as she left. "I'll stop by tomorrow after work."

"Sounds good."

Chris turned his attention to the phone call.

"Hi there. How are you doing?" Candace asked.

"Pretty good. I may get out of here in two days, the doctor said. How is your trip going?"

"I got a few minutes to talk. I have a dinner meeting with a client and just wanted to check in. How is it going at the house?"

"The older two have been lukewarm to me but my youngest, Jennifer, seems happy to see me."

"Those two never seem to appreciate all you do for them. They live in a nice house and have all the things they want. I know how hard you work. Don't they appreciate that?" Candace said with disgust.

"Look, I may be a little at fault with this too."

"Is that what your ex, Liz, is telling you? Don't listen to her. She's just bitter about the divorce and how you have moved on with your life, and she's stuck with the kids."

"It's Elizabeth and can we just leave that whole topic alone for now?"

"You're right. So, the operation went well?"

"Yes, things went fine. The surgeon thought the polyp is benign, but we need to confirm with the biopsy results."

"Hey, I must go. My client has arrived for dinner. I'll talk with you tomorrow. Love you."

"OK. Talk with you tomorrow." Christopher said with exasperation from the whole conversation.

Chris had problems going to sleep and watched cable news for awhile. A nurse came in around 4 am to check his vital signs and give him a few medications.

"If you have any pain, there's a morphine dispenser tied into your IV that you can use on demand. Don't worry, there is a limit to how much you can take in each period. Also, your doctor wants you to walk a little bit before he sees you in the morning."

"That shouldn't be too hard, since I can now feel my legs again after the surgery."

"Well, just in case, I'll help you up," the nurse said.

She took off the compression cuffs from his legs and helped him sit up in bed. Chris discovered he was very shaky getting up and trying to walk. With help from the nurse, he was able to walk a few feet to a nearby chair and then sat down to rest. He got a little nauseous, and the nurse got him a patch and placed it behind his ear.

"This should clear that up. It's the same thing people take for sea sickness," she assured him.

"Wow, that was much harder than I expected," Chris told her.

"That's why I helped you out. It's perfectly normal after surgery."

With help from the nurse, Chris got back into bed, the compression cuffs were put back on, and he managed to doze off for a couple of hours.

NINETEEN

Chris awoke to the sound of a loud beeping noise.

"What the heck is that noise?" Chris asked the nurse who entered the room anxiously.

"It's an alarm indicating your heart rate is above 120 beats per minute," she replied calmly as she checked his blood pressure.

"I don't feel anything in my chest like my heart beating very fast. Maybe the clip on my finger is not working properly," Chris replied.

"Well, we'll keep an eye on it this morning and see what your doctor wants to do if it continues."

Later his doctor arrived to check in on him.

"So, how are you feeling today?" he asked Chris as he looked over his charts at the foot of the bed.

"OK, considering everything."

"I see you have had episodes of elevated heart rates this morning. Do you have any sort of heart arrhythmia?"

"Not that I know of," Chris replied, wondering where this conversation was going.

"Just to be sure it's nothing more than a result of some dehydration, let's have an EKG done."

A few minutes later, a nurse came in and placed about a dozen electrodes with circular adhesive tape at different locations on his body. A few moments later she tore off a paper strip and left the room. She returned saying there were no problems, and the doctor said to increase the IV fluids.

"Your doctor thought you may be dehydrated from taking two bowel preps in less than two weeks and not drinking fluids for a day since your surgery," she told him as she hung another bag on the IV hook. "That should take care of you for a while. I will be back later to remove your catheter. Your bladder seems to be doing well based on how fast you're filling the bag."

"I can't wait for that event," Chris said sarcastically as she left.

Later that morning the nurse returned to remove the catheter. Chris expected a lot of discomfort with the procedure but was surprised how little sensation there was. A couple of hours later he found that he couldn't urinate even though his bladder was full. The nurse used an ultrasound to confirm his bladder was full. She asked for his surgeon to discuss the situation.

"This happens sometimes after surgery. The bladder takes a little time to get functioning properly. So, while we wait, you'll get a temporary catheterization just to drain the bladder," his doctor explained.

"You're going to do that while I'm awake?" Chris asked, terrified of what was going to take place.

"No problem. I've done these many times," the nurse assured him.

After the doctor left, the nurse quickly performed the catheterization and said he would feel better soon. At this point, Chris thought, *Just get on with it so I can get some relief.* The pain was getting almost unbearable, and he didn't care about any discomfort from the procedure. After filling another bag, the catheter was removed, and Chris felt much better and hoped he would be able to urinate on his own the next time.

A couple of hours later, Chris was back to normal. He couldn't believe how much he took routine things for granted.

Chris settled in his bed and watched some news and fell asleep. Later in the afternoon, his children and Elizabeth stopped by for a visit.

"Hey, Dad, how are you doing?" Jennifer asked later that afternoon.

"OK. It's nice to see everyone here. I never saw this coming, but I appreciate being able to spend some time with you. Jennifer, Pastor Jim stopped by before my surgery to say hello. He said you asked him to come by."

"Yes, I did. I thought you could use the company."

"Thanks. I did appreciate his visit. I'd like to talk more about Lakeside Church with you while I'm home."

"That would be great. I'd love to have you attend a service there too," she replied with excitement.

"We'll see. So how are you two doing?"

"School is boring as usual," John said.

"My friends invited me to a party this weekend. Mom is not sure about letting me go. What do you think?" Sarah asked.

"I'll discuss this with your mother. However, since she's with you all the time, I trust her judgment more than mine!" Christopher said with a smile as he saw a divide and conquer approach with Sarah on this one.

"Thanks for the vote of confidence," Elizabeth said, pleasantly surprised by his reply to Sarah. "It's getting late, and you all have homework to do, and I need to get dinner going. I'll see you tomorrow."

"Sounds good and I hope to be discharged tomorrow. See you all later."

Pastor Jim stopped by to see how Chris was doing later in the evening.

"How are you feeling?" Pastor Jim asked as he stuck his head through the doorway into the room.

"OK, all things considered."

"Do you mind if I stop by for a little while?"

"Not at all, I got plenty of time on my hands."

Pastor Jim pulled up a chair to sit next to Chris's bed.

"There is something I would like to discuss with you," Chris said seriously, starting the conversation.

"Sure. What's on your mind?"

"My daughter Jennifer is really involved with your church youth group. She's even talking about getting baptized and has given her life to Christ. I don't know what to make of this. I know I haven't been around much, but church has not been part of our family life and suddenly Jennifer is 'all in with Jesus.'"

"I like that phrase, 'all in with Jesus.' You know, that's the way it is sometimes with Jesus. Once you meet Him, you can't live without Him. Jessica Chambers invited Jennifer to come to our youth group meetings last year. She was really having problems with the divorce and not sure how to fit into life anymore. She discovered other kids like her in similar situations. Unfortunately, divorced families are much too common, even among Christians. We're not perfect either."

"What does she see in Jesus?" Chris asked. "I have got to admit, I never felt like He was very close to me. I remember going to church as a kid, but it was something we just did on Sundays and didn't think much about the rest of the week. Ev-

eryone just went out of habit and maybe to be socially acceptable."

"Well, that's part of what's different in this church. We
encourage everyone to serve others outside of the church,
which is what Jesus did. Christ felt compassion for the outcasts
of the society of his time. It's the same today with kids like
Jennifer that feel rejected and outcast; even if she isn't, it's the
way she feels. Jesus knows how she feels and accepts her as she
is. This is what she finds attractive about Christ and makes
Him a part of her daily life. She knows Jesus won't let her
down."

"Like I let her down?" Chri asked quietly.

"I didn't say that. Do you think you let her down?"

"I don't know. At the time, it seemed like the right thing
to do. Her mom and I just argued all the time and never could
agree on anything. We seemed to have different goals. I honestly thought the kids would do better without their mom and
dad always arguing and yelling at each other. It's too late to rethink those decisions. Elizabeth and I have moved on, and the
kids need to accept that fact."

"Do you really think nothing can be changed? Remember
what I told you about with God all things are possible."

"Not with me. Since I don't even believe in God, I guess
He won't help me much."

"I wouldn't be so sure about that. I believe God works
through people to do His will. Perhaps Jennifer is being used
by God to get to you."

"I find that hard to believe. Besides, why would God care
about my situation? I'm not even a believer. I'm sure there are
plenty of Christians that could use His help."

"God cares about everyone," Pastor Jim responded. "Jesus

said, "There will be more rejoicing in heaven over one sinner who repents than over ninety-nine righteous persons who do not need to repent (Luke 15:7).

"That doesn't sound like the way things work down here. No one is looking out for you except yourself. I see that all the time at work. In fact, I may lose out on a big promotion because I'm stuck here in a hospital room and not closing an important deal in Europe."

"There may be a bigger deal going on here, but only God sees the whole picture. We only see what's happening around us and not from God's perspective. In 2 Corinthians 4:18 the Apostle Paul writes 'So we fix our eyes not on what is seen, but on what is unseen, since what is seen is temporary, but what is unseen is eternal.'"

"You know that verse from memory?"

"Yes, I find certain verses from the scriptures resonate with me enough that I want to remember them. They sometimes are helpful in certain situations."

"I never read the Bible. I don't think it's very relevant to my life or this time. It was written a long time ago, and a lot has changed."

"People haven't changed," Pastor Jim said, "and the Bible is about God's relationship with us, not current events. Paul is saying that we need to focus on what God's plan is for our lives, not what we see going on around us. Some of what is happening here may be part of a much bigger plan God has for us."

"So, having part of my colon removed may be part of God's bigger plan for me?"

"It might be God's way of putting you here with your family, at least for a while. Or He will use this situation for His plan in some way. They may need you more than you need to be in Los Angeles. This may also be true for you."

"Well, I guess I have some time to think about all of this."

"Yes, you do, about 40 days, in fact. Hey, I got to go, but I'll keep you in my prayers."

"Thanks for stopping by. I'll talk with Jennifer more about her new-found faith."

"I think you'll find that very revealing if you keep your mind and heart open to the Holy Spirit."

"What's that about?"

"That's a part of God within all Christians who guides us, if we take the time to listen. I believe He's guiding Jennifer. Have a good night and get better soon."

"Will do," Chris said as the pastor got up from his chair and left the room.

Chris stared at the wall while thinking about his conversation with Pastor Jim. *How could God be working through Jennifer to reach me? What does He want? My life is going along fine now. I have a great job and a gorgeous girlfriend. I have a great life in LA. How could God improve on this?*

Chris decided to watch a baseball game to get his mind off these seemingly foreign thoughts about God having a purpose and plan for his life. He fell asleep before the end of the game. He was awakened around four in the morning by the same nurse he saw the previous night. She checked his vital signs and drew more blood.

"Are you ready for another walk?" she asked Chris.

"Yes, I think I'm doing a lot better tonight than last night."

"Great, I'll help you put on your robe over your gown."

She helped put his robe on and stayed with him as they

walked around the hall with the IV pole going with them. After he got back to the room, she helped him get the robe off, and he got back in the bed very slowly. He was now feeling sore from the incision when he bent his torso. However, he was surprised that it didn't feel much worse than a very sore muscle. After settling into bed, he watched an early morning cable news program and drifted off to sleep.

When he awoke a few hours later, the nurse asked him what he would like for breakfast. She handed him a low residue diet menu.

"I guess I need to start getting used to this diet in a couple of weeks. I'll go with eggs, toast, and juice," he said as he noticed this meant scrambled eggs, plain white bread, and pulp-free juice.

Elizabeth came into the room while he was eating.

"This is a surprise! I didn't expect to see you until tonight," Chris said, happy to see her.

"Well, your surgeon said you may be able to leave today, and I thought I'd stop in to see how you were doing."

"I'm glad you stopped by. What do you think of my breakfast?"

"It actually looks reasonable. I wasn't sure what your diet would look like."

A little while later, his surgeon knocked on the door.

"Well, it looks like you're good to go," the surgeon told Christopher. "Just take it easy at home, don't lift anything more than ten pounds, and follow the low residue diet I gave you for at least two weeks. Assuming you are off any pain medications, you can drive after two weeks."

"That sounds great. Let's get out of here!" Christopher told Elizabeth as his doctor was leaving the room.

"Listen, why don't you use Jennifer's bedroom for a while? I think it will be easier to get in and out of bed than from the couch," Elizabeth suggested as Chris struggled to get out of bed. He still had some pain from the three incisions with the laparoscopic surgery. "She had offered her room before you got here. I admit I was not happy with you coming to stay, and so I decided to let you have the couch."

"No problem. I understand how you feel. I would probably do the same. I think I will take up Jennifer's generous offer to make life easier for myself. Where will she stay?"

"She will use the futon in the finished basement. There's a TV and full bath there, and she'll be fine."

"Now that's settled, get changed out of that hospital gown into these sweats you brought with you before surgery. I'll carry your duffle bag while you get brought to the car in a wheel-chair."

"I hate to admit it, but that forty days' thing has been stuck in my head," Christopher told her.

"Forget it. It would take a miracle to fix our family problems and maybe even forty years."

TWENTY

When Chris and Elizabeth arrived home, she helped him get out of the car. His abdominal muscles were sore when he stretched and bent as he got out of the car. *The neighborhood was quiet in the middle of the afternoon,* he thought when he was home in the middle of the day. He didn't recall being home sick very often. It felt strange to him not to be at work in the middle of the day.

"I bet you never thought you would care for me! That's only supposed to happen if we grow old together," Chris said sarcastically as Elizabeth grabbed his arm to help him ease slowly out of the passenger seat.

"Well, I guess we're growing older together whether we like it or not. The kids certainly are getting older regardless of what we do or don't do. Let's get you settled inside, and I'll go back and get your bag.

Once inside the house, Chris sat down in a wingback chair that he didn't remember being there when he had first arrived before his surgery. The house was quiet except for Toby who was running around the family room excited to see Chris.

"Where did this chair come from?" he asked Elizabeth.

"I found it downstairs and thought it would be easier for

you to get up and down from since it is higher and stiffer than the couches in the room. It was in the living room a long time ago. I put a slipcover over it since it had a few worn spots."

"That was very thoughtful of you. I might think you even care about me a little bit," Chris said in a suggestive tone.

"You're a guest here and my children's father so I should treat you well, I suppose," Elizabeth said with small smile. "Now that you're settled here, I'll get dinner started before the kids get home."

"Sounds good to me. I'll check out any sports on TV that are on in the middle of the afternoon on a weekday. Maybe I can catch part of a golf tournament. I usually only see the weekend portions of tournaments."

While keeping Chris' low residue diet in mind, Elizabeth looked at the suggested dinner menu and food selections Chris received when he was discharged from the hospital. He needed to avoid all raw vegetables and other foods that are difficult to digest for at least two weeks.

For breakfast, he could have scrambled eggs, yogurt, Rice Krispies, white bread, or English muffins. For lunch, he can have well-cooked sliced deli meats such as ham, turkey, or chicken. Cheeses include American, cheddar, and Swiss. Plain white bread or white hamburger buns were allowed. For dinners, he could have well-cooked tender beef and poultry, among other meats. Rice and pasta were also allowed. All these foods were to be served in small portions.

As she and Chris would learn over time, he had a very small appetite and would stick with Rice Krispies and white toast for breakfast, deli chicken for lunch, and pasta for dinner. He started losing weight, bottoming out at twenty pounds less than his pre-surgery weight.

She decided to go with spaghetti and meatballs for supper. The kids always liked this, and Chris could at least eat the spaghetti, if not the meatballs.

Chris ate a small portion at dinner, like a small plate served in some restaurants. After dinner, Chris headed for the family room to watch some of the evening news in the wingback chair. Elizabeth joined him after cleaning up the kitchen from dinner.

"Thanks for the spaghetti dinner. I see you reviewed my low residue diet. I still wasn't very hungry. The doctor told me that it may take a while for my digestive system to wake up and be working as usual," Chris told Elizabeth as she settled on the couch nearby.

"I'm glad to help with your diet. I'll get some food items listed on the menu for breakfast and lunch tomorrow after work. I think there are enough food items here that you can eat until I stock up tomorrow."

"I'm sure there are, especially with the amount I'm eating. Thanks again for having me here and for letting me use Jennifer's room. I know this is a big disruption in your life and the kids' lives, especially after your getting settled into life after our divorce."

"It may surprise you, but we haven't really settled into life after our divorce," Elizabeth shared. "It may look like we have, but as I told you the kids are having a lot of problems, and I'm having problems dealing with all their problems."

Chris took a moment to think about what she said. He felt a little guilty that he had moved on and was not dealing with the kids' problems, leaving all that to Elizabeth. He thought about how being with Candace made him feel a lot younger and helped him forget about his family back in Chicago.

"I'm here for six weeks, let's see what happens. I'll try my best to reconnect with them. I realize I haven't been around and left all this to you," he said candidly.

Elizabeth looked at Chris, surprised at his total admission and plain honesty about the situation. She was not sure what to say.

"I appreciate that. At this point I'll take any help I can get, even for only six weeks, which I believe is not nearly enough time to fix things around here. It's getting late, and I need to get up to go to work in the morning. Someone must make a living around here," she said as she stood up and headed for her bedroom.

Chris decided to stay up and watch TV for awhile and think about how he might be able to help his estranged family while he was there. He fell asleep in the chair and went to bed after waking up around two in the morning.

TWENTY-ONE

Chris spent the next day getting accustomed to being at home all day by himself. He started to think about getting into some kind of routine each day. He was used to having someone else set up his daily schedule of meetings but now it was up to him to fill in the eight or ten hours that made up the usual workday he had become accustomed to.

Elizabeth was back at work and got a call from Samantha.

"Hey, are you available for lunch today?" she asked Elizabeth.

"I need to catch up after taking yesterday off to get Chris home from the hospital and settled in."

"How is he doing?"

"He's all right. He doesn't seem to be having much pain from the incision and stays up late watching sports or cable news."

"I give you credit for taking him in for several weeks. I would have told him to let his girlfriend take care of him. It sounds like she is there only for the good times."

"I don't know how serious they are, but I think the marriage vows still say something about being there in sickness and in health," Elizabeth said with a laugh not sure why she was joking about Chris' latest relationship. She thought that maybe it helped her deal with his moving on.

"Well, let me know if I can be of any help."

"Will do," Elizabeth said as she ended the call and was looking at her email inbox. She couldn't believe how much email had piled up in a day.

The kids started to arrive home from school later that day.

"Hi, Dad," John said as he entered the house and saw Christopher sitting in the wingback chair watching a golf tournament on television. "How's it going being at home all day?"

"All right, for now. I haven't been home long enough to be bored yet. So, how was school today?"

"Unlike what you said, I have been there long enough to be bored."

"How's that?"

"I don't see how anything they teach is relevant for me."

"In what way?"

"I just don't see the point. Like what am I going to do with all this math stuff?"

"Well, you can at least use it to figure out what a loan will cost in terms of interest or how much material you may need for a project at home."

"Maybe, but I don't know what use most of the classes are."

"Have you thought about what you want to do after high school?"

"Not really. Most of my friends don't have any plans either."

"Why is that?"

"I don't know. I just haven't thought that far ahead."

"It's only next year. When are you going to start thinking about it?" Christopher replied with some irritation in his voice.

"I don't know! Why do you even care? It's not like you discuss this with me regularly!"

"I'm your father, and I do care. I admit I have not been very involved with you and your siblings the last few years. Do any of your friends plan on going to college?"

"Not really. College is for nerds and preppies. They either want to go into stuff like engineering and science or just party all week at college."

"How do you plan on making a living?"

"I haven't thought about it much. Maybe I can get a job at the mall."

"That's no kind of career. That's for high school kids. You need to start taking on some accountability for yourself."

"Well, who are you accountable to?"

"Look, regardless of what you think about me, I have always supported you and the rest of the family. That didn't just happen. I got good grades in high school, went to college, and then to graduate school and got an MBA. With that I've been able to make a good living. I'm not independently wealthy so I can't support you as an adult. You will need to support yourself."

"Yeah, yeah. I get it. I'll figure something out. I just need some time."

"Time is what you have very little of left. What do you like doing? If you work at something you like, you'll most likely be successful."

"Is that what this is all about? Me being a success like you?

Maybe I just can't measure up to your standards," John replied defiantly.

"That's not true. Besides, it's not about measuring up to anyone's standards. It's about doing something you like and being successful at it. You have great capabilities. I remember how well you did in grade school and junior high. You really liked school then. You talked about being an astronaut when you grew up. What happened?"

"You and Mom got divorced is what happened. After you left, Mom was not herself. She would get upset at the smallest thing. She didn't seem interested in what I was doing. She got more wrapped up in her job. So, I guess I just lost interest in school and thinking about the future."

"I didn't know your mother felt that way. She never said anything to me."

"Did you ever ask how she's doing? Hey, I must meet up with some friends. Tell Mom I won't be home for dinner," John said with disgust after getting no reply from Christopher to his question and left the room.

John met up with his friend Bob at the mall.

"How are things going at home with your dad?" Bob asked John as they were walking around the mall with some other guys, checking out the girls.

"I got into a boring discussion on what I want to do when I grow up. He seems all concerned about my future. I told him I would figure it out later."

"My parents are starting to bug me about this stuff too. What's the big deal? We got our whole lives to worry about that kind of stuff. Right now, I want to worry about asking this hot girl in my history class to this Saturday's party. My friend's parents will be away for the weekend, and he's in charge of the house. I'm sure I could get you in if you are interested."

"That would be great. I could use a change of scenery after my dad being around all week."

"Great, now let's check out these girls that just passed by us. I think they're from our school. Maybe we can invite them to the party."

TWENTY-TWO

How did your day go?" Sarah asked Christopher the next afternoon.

"Same as the past few days; I'm starting to get a taste for what retirement looks like!"

"You aren't ready to retire." She laughed at the thought.

"After a few days sitting on a couch or chair watching TV, I'm definitely certain I'm not ready to retire. So how are things going with you? I can't believe you're in high school."

"School's going OK. My classes are easy. Mom said I should consider honors classes next year."

"I agree with your mother. You should challenge yourself more."

"I can get by with easy classes, why bother working more? I'd rather hang out with my friends and go to parties than study."

"Why do you want to go to parties?"

"It's what all the kids do."

"All of them?"

"Well, at least the fun students. The rest are boring and not fun to hang around. They spend a lot of time either studying or practicing for sports."

"But you're one of the smart students at the school. Why isn't that enough?"

"Well, I may be, but I don't want my friends to know that. They would dump me in a second."

"Why is that?"

"They don't want anything to do with those other kids. At lunch time, we all just hang out together. Some of my friends will make jokes about other students in the lunchroom."

"You never used to do those kinds of things. In fact, you used to sit with students at lunch time that didn't have friends when you were in junior high school."

"Well, things change. I don't want to be with those kids anymore. I want to have a good time with my friends," she said with a serious look on her face.

"Look, you're a very smart girl with lots of opportunities ahead. Do you ever think about what you might like to do as an adult?"

"Sometimes; but I like being accepted by the in-crowd at school. I never was before, and I like the attention."

"What does your mother say about all this?"

"Not much. She's busy with work and getting home in time to get dinner on. We don't talk very much."

"I guess I haven't been around to talk with either."

"That's OK. I know you have your work to do in LA, and that's important. I heard from Mom you may be up for a promotion."

"Yes, that's right. Before this surgery came up, I was scheduled for an important trip to Europe to close a deal on a new business. That would probably guarantee the promotion."

"So, what happens while you are away?"

"Someone else will complete the deal."

"Will they get the promotion?"

"Who knows?"

"I hope you still get it. I know this is important to you."

"After talking with you and John, I'm starting to wonder what is important! I think dinner is nearly ready so we should help your mother set the table."

"Sure. Hey, Dad—I kind of liked talking with you."

"Me too," he replied with a smile.

TWENTY-THREE

ow was school today?" Christopher asked Jennifer as she came into the living room. As usual he was watching a sports program in the middle of the afternoon,

"Great. I like my classes, and the teachers seem to be really interested in help us learn."

"Wow! That's quite a different response than I get from your brother and sister about high school."

"I know they seem to not like school very much. Maybe high school is different with so many students, and the teachers may be much busier than in junior high school."

"Well, maybe. So, besides school, what else do you like doing?"

"I'm on the girls Lacrosse team."

"That can be pretty hard hitting at times."

"Yea, but I love running the field, and I have a good time with the players. We go out to the mall or movies on weekends or just hang out at one of their houses."

"That sounds great. Hey, can you tell me more about your church activities?

"Sure. What do you want to know?"

"How did you get interested?"

"I hate to tell you this, but after you and Mom got divorced, I was depressed. One of my teammates is Jessica Chambers, our neighbor. I started talking to her about how I felt. She said she couldn't imagine what it would be like if her parents got divorced, but she wanted to try to help me any way she could."

"I didn't realize how this affected you. You should have said something to me or your mom."

"You and Mom seemed to be having enough problems, and I didn't want to add to them," Jennifer explained. "So, after a while, Jessica invited me to her church youth group meeting. At first, I said I wasn't interested but after thinking about it for a while, I decided to go and see what it was all about. They're a group of guys and girls that hang out together and play games. That day they had a pick-up softball game. Afterwards we had a barbeque and sat around a campfire at night just talking about things.

"I decided to keep going to the youth group events. After a while, Jessica invited me to the youth service at their church. Pastor Jim led this service just for junior and senior high students. He seemed nice and talked about how the Bible and Jesus are relevant to our daily lives.

"Some weeks, he talked about family problems and how Jesus could help us deal with them. Well, at one service, he talked about dealing with divorce. It was like he was talking directly to me! I finally started to feel better about myself. He said that God has a purpose and a plan for each of our lives, and no matter what we are going through, He is always there, even if we feel all alone."

"So, did you feel alone?" Christopher asked with concern and surprise in his voice.

"Yes, I did. Well, I started to pray about all this stuff and decided to accept Jesus Christ as my Lord and Savior. Just doing that didn't change things, but it did change the way I dealt with them. I then started to wonder why we never went to church."

"That's a hard question to answer. Your mom and I went to church as kids and were even baptized. As we got older, church just didn't seem relevant to any parts of our lives. So, we never really gave it much thought. So, accepting Jesus as your Lord and Savior really has affected your life?"

"It sure has. Like I said, I still sometimes get depressed, and things haven't changed suddenly. But I do believe God can change people."

"That's funny you said that. Pastor Jim told me that at the hospital. He said He could do it in as little as 40 days!"

"I believe He can do it instantly if He wants. Pastor Jim told the story of Saul being converted from persecuting Christians to being renamed Paul and becoming a leader of the Church instantly. This happened when he saw Jesus while he was traveling on the road to Damascus."

"Well, I guess I might want to rethink Jesus and God while I'm here."

"It wouldn't hurt. Maybe you'll become a follower like Paul."

"Now, that would truly take a miracle!"

"Well, I believe miracles still happen."

After Jennifer left, Chris thought back on a childhood memory about a friend of his that had cancer.

I remember my friend Jimmy getting sick and missing a lot of school. His family lived near me. My parents used to talk with them about him when we would see them in the neighborhood. They went to church regularly, and they talked about praying for their son to get better. Instead, he just kept getting worse. I remember not seeing him at all after a while. Finally, one day, my parents told me he had died. At the wake, I remember his mother being very angry at God and asking why He would let this happen. No one had an answer. So, I guess I really don't believe in miracles. At least I have not seen one yet.

TWENTY-FOUR

As Chris was still thinking about Jimmy and his childhood, his cell phone rang and abruptly jogged him back to the present.

"Hi Sam, how are things going?" Christopher asked.

"Things are going along OK here. Joe was assigned to cover for you while you're away. He had good meetings with your clients last week. By the way, they wished you a speedy recovery. How are you doing?"

"I'm coming along. I'm a little sore from the incisions, one about three inches and the other two about a half inch each. I'm also on a low fiber diet or low residue diet, so I have somewhat limited food choices. I really don't have much of an appetite either, so I have been losing weight.

"How is it being at your ex's house?"

"Not as bad as I thought it would be. I'm catching up with my kids. Some are doing better than others. I didn't realize how hard the divorce has been on them."

"Don't worry about the kids. They bounce back and will do fine. What you should be worrying about is the deal in Europe. Joe is getting briefed on it by management and will be heading out next week. I overheard him talking with some of the guys here. He thought he could become a front runner for the executive VP job if he closes the deal."

"That's what I was afraid of. As they say, 'out of sight, out of mind.' I have seen this when people retire. No matter how high the job level, a couple of weeks after they're gone, things are moving along like they never existed."

"As another saying goes, 'no one is irreplaceable.'"

"You got that right. I can't believe I may be passed up for that promotion. I laid all the groundwork for that deal. Now, someone out of nowhere is going to take it away from me!"

"Hey, settle down. That may not happen. This guy is just purely guessing. Our president, Don, knows how valuable you are to the organization."

"I'm not so sure. He was hoping I would put off this surgery until after the deal was completed. I got the impression I should be putting the company first, even ahead of my health."

"I can't believe that. He was probably just frustrated with the sudden change of plans. You know he is a control freak and can't handle surprises."

"Maybe, but I would appreciate a little more support from management."

"Just focus on getting well and don't worry about work."

"I'll try, but I sacrificed a lot for that job, and I hate to see it fall apart due to things I can't control. I specifically took this job because of the advancement opportunity. I had it all figured out. With my divorce, I was free to do whatever I wanted. I couldn't have taken this job when I was married. Elizabeth had her job in Chicago, and she would have never agreed to have the kids move from Chicago. They have all their friends there."

"You are also a control freak. Just relax and get some rest," Sam said with an encouraging tone in his voice.

"OK, you're right, I'll check in next week."

TWENTY-FIVE

Chris decided to lay down on the couch in the family room and rest for a while. He tried to take his mind off what was happening at work while he was away. He slowly went to sleep. After about a couple of hours, he woke up and decided to call Candace.

"Hi Candace. I thought I'd check in with you," Christopher said, thinking he hadn't heard from her in a couple of days.

"Hey there. I've been meaning to call you. I've been traveling, and time just goes by so fast. I'm back in LA for now. How are you feeling?"

"I'm coming along. I'm a little sore from the incisions and not very hungry. The doctor told me both are normal. In fact, I could lose up to twenty pounds before I get back on a normal diet."

"I guess we should eat out a lot to get our weight back. How are things with Liz and the kids?"

"That's Elizabeth, and things are going OK. I'm finding out how hard my divorce has been on the kids. They all have been dealing with it in different ways. The most surprising was Jennifer is now going to a church my old neighbors go to."

"I'd be careful about any churches. They may try to change her thinking and may even convert her to following Jesus."

"That's exactly what has happened."

"You better be careful that those church folks don't start bad mouthing you for divorcing their mother. You needed to get out of that relationship. Your kids will do fine. They're just whiners. I hear this from other friends who have gotten divorced."

"From what I hear, I don't think anyone at that church is talking negatively about me or Elizabeth. They seem to be helping Jennifer cope with the whole thing. I'm not sure my kids are whining. They have been getting into some serious problems. John will be lucky to graduate, and Sarah is hanging with the wrong crowd."

"You shouldn't have to worry about that stuff. Your ex has custody of the kids. That's her problem. You give them plenty of money for child support, and all she must do is keep an eye on the kids. You do plenty for them. Some of my friends who are divorced have kids that don't get a dime from their ex's. You do more than most of them."

"I don't know. There just seems to be a lot of problems here."

"Your family is no different than most. I've got to go to a meeting now. I'll talk with you later. Love you," Candace said ending the call before Christopher had a chance to reply.

Chris thought back to when he and Candace had started dating.

"I had a great time seeing Hollywood. The tour guide did a nice job telling all those stories about the stars and their homes," he had told Candace as they sat down for dinner at the Proud Bird that night. "Those tours of Hollywood are popular with the tourists. I'm not sure if the stars like all the attention in their neighborhoods."

"I figure that's the price they pay for being celebrities," she replied.

"I guess you're right. I did feel just like those tourists and forgot I live here now!"

"So, how do you like LA since you moved here?"

"It's a lot different than when I used to travel here on business. I would fly into LAX and get a rental car or cab to get to a downtown hotel. I never dealt with the interstate highways, like I do now. Living in Valencia I must go on the interstates every day, and the traffic is terrible."

"You just have to get up early and leave at 4 AM to miss the rush hour," Candace suggested.

"No way, I am not a morning person. So how do you like your job?"

"It's OK for a first job. I want to get on the fast track and probably will be looking for another job after I get enough experience to put it on my resume. I see you may be on the short list for a high-level job here," Candace said with a sly smile on her face.

"Well, I admit the prospect of a high-level position attracted me here. After my divorce, I was free to move as I wish."

"Being single does have its advantages. How old are your kids?"

"One in grade school, two in junior high school."

"Three kids, I can't imagine having any kids. They would just get in the way of my career. I'd have to worry about day care and take days off when they're sick. You guys never have to worry about that stuff. It seems to always be the wife who needs to take care of the kids."

"How do you figure that?"

"I see some of the women at work with kids. It doesn't matter what job they have; they always must take care of the kids. Some have complained about their husbands not doing much with the kids."

"You know this is a great restaurant with a nice view of LAX. It's kind of relaxing watching the airplanes land and take off," Chris said to change the subject. Her comments hit a little too close to home for him.

"The food is good here. So, did you grow up in Chicago?"

"No, I grew up in Holyoke, Massachusetts. It's nothing like Chicago or LA. It's a working-class town. My father and mother just had high school diplomas. My father is a World War II vet and got a job in the same town he grew up in after the war. So, I'm the first generation to go to college."

"I have got to admit I grew up in what I guess would be an upper-class family in Newport Beach," Candace explained. "My dad is an executive in a large company, and my mom went to a high-priced private school majoring in finding a rich guy. I hung out at the family summer home on Catalina Island most summers while I was at USC. I got to admit, I'm impressed you really had to work hard for everything you have."

Wow, this sounds just like my ex-wife's biography! Chris thought with disbelief. *I seem to be attracted to women from affluent backgrounds. Maybe that's my problem with relationships.*

"So where did you go to college?" she asked him.

"I went to the University of Massachusetts, a large state college. It's a good school but a lot less expensive than private schools. Even that was a financial challenge for my family, so I worked every summer to help with the costs. I got a degree in business administration and started a job in the Boston area. I then went to Harvard Business School and got an MBA."

"So, I guess I can claim I am dating a Harvard man?" Candice said with a smile and a bit of sarcasm in her voice.

"Please don't say that. That will really make me feel old."

"I don't think you're old. I do think people can think they are old, and then they are old."

"So, you don't think I'm old?"

"Not at all, just mature. How long have you been divorced?"

"A couple of years and I have been in LA for about six months and decided it was time to move on with life. This is the first date I've had since about twenty years ago."

"I'm honored to be your first date," Candace said as she raised her glass of wine. "Here's to new beginnings."

"I agree," Chris said as he and Candace finished the toast and clanged their glasses.

Chris was once again brought back to the present with Elizabeth telling him and the kids that dinner was ready.

"So how are things going for you here?" Elizabeth asked as she and Christopher were having coffee after cleaning up the kitchen.

"I'm not sure where to begin. I have had time to talk with the kids and catch up with them. John doesn't know what he wants to do after high school; that is, if he graduates. Sarah is doing well with school but is gravitating towards the wrong crowd. Jennifer has become a Jesus freak but at least appears to be doing well with school and has a good group of friends. A guy named Joe is taking over my job and will probably steal my promotion. Does that sum things up well?"

"It sounds like you quickly got up to speed with things around here. I'm not sure about the Joe situation," Elizabeth added in a sarcastic tone to lighten things up. "Let's discuss one kid at a time."

"That sounds reasonable to me."

"Let's start with John. He has become very aloof. He barely talks to me anymore. I try to talk with him after dinner, but he usually just heads right out of the house with friends, who I know little about. I don't know when I last saw him do any homework."

"I tried to talk with him about some of these things, but he just shut me off too," Chris told her. "He even said I don't care because I left for LA. I wonder if he may have a point. It's hard to keep close relationships when I live a couple of thousand miles away," he said thoughtfully.

"Well, that was your choice. I wasn't very happy with your decision to leave Chicago, but I thought if we're divorced, you can do whatever you wish," Elizabeth replied sharply.

"That was sort of the theme in our marriage too," Chris said. "You did what you wanted, and I did what I wanted, especially with our careers."

"A long time ago I would have argued with you about whose career came first," Elizabeth admitted. "But now I realize we were both guilty on that one. At any rate, I have trouble trying to keep my job going and taking care of the children. I should have tried harder with John, but by the end of the day, I just don't have enough energy left. He does need help. He's going on a path leading to nowhere.

"Sarah is doing OK right now. She's at a critical point in her life. She still has interest in school and careers after high school in terms of going to college. However, she has been starting to get interested in hanging out with girls who are popular but not for the right reasons. I think she has low self-esteem, and these girls make her feel good about herself. I'm not sure why she has this. She's smart and attractive, so she doesn't need these kids. She has always been successful up to now, and there's no reason for her not to be successful in high school."

"High school can be intimidating. Maybe with all the family problems, she has lost all confidence in herself. I sensed that when talking with her," Christopher added.

"You may be right. I remember being intimidated when I was in high school by the large number of students and classes. Maybe you can talk with her while you're here?" Elizabeth was hopeful.

"I'll try to do this. Now, what about Jennifer? She seems to have taken another path that I don't understand, but it has seemed to be working for her."

"I agree. I'm not sure about all this Christian stuff, but she's doing better than the other kids, and she has a good group of friends. In addition, we both know Paul and Linda Chambers well, and I trust them. If they're associated with this church, I'm comfortable with that."

"I agree. Paul and Linda have always been good friends of ours, and I'm fine with Jennifer being involved in their church. Have you thought much about getting active in a church your-self?"

"Not really. John and Sarah don't seem interested, and this would be just another thing to drag them to. I have enough problems with getting John to school these days! As you now see, I have my work cut out for me with the kids."

"Not just you, but us. I'm starting to appreciate what you have been dealing with. I'll see what I can do. I've only been here a few weeks and can't promise a miracle, although Pastor Jim would say that is plenty of time," Chris said with a smile.

They both laughed at this. Chris couldn't remember the last time he and Elizabeth shared a good laugh about anything. It had been a long time…

The next day, Chris heard from his doctor about the biopsy results.

"Hi Chris, this is Dr. Peterson," he said as Chris answered his cell phone. Chris was understandably nervous about the results, although everything looked good.

"Hi, Dr. Peterson, I assume you're calling about my biopsy results."

"Yes, I have good news. The test results are all normal, no cancer present."

"That's great news. I must admit, I've been concerned about the results, even though things looked OK."

"Also, I called to see how you're feeling."

"I'm doing OK. I've been a little sore but have not needed the Vicodin."

"That's good to hear. Just keep on the low residue diet for the next couple of weeks, and you should be fine."

"Will do."

"Great, I'll see you in a few weeks," Dr. Peterson said as he ended the call.

Later that day, Chris told Elizabeth about the test results.

"Hey, how did your day go?" Elizabeth asked Chris as she came in after work.

"Really well! My doctor called me and said the biopsy results were negative for any cancer."

"That is good news!" Elizabeth said with genuine relief. "Even though we thought things were OK, I guess I was a little concerned."

"Me too. You know, this whole thing has gotten me thinking about how I have spent my life. If I did have colon cancer, who knows if I would be around next year."

"Let's not go there. Let's just be thankful for the good outcome," she said seriously.

"I agree. However, I'll at least see what I can do to make things better with our kids and my relationship with them while I'm here."

"I think that sounds like a good start," Elizabeth said as she considered her own life to date and what she could have done differently.

Chris called Candice late that evening to tell her the good news.

"Hi, Candace, I wanted to tell you about the test results," Chris said as he started the conversation.

"You heard today?"

"Yea. Everything is fine."

"That's great news, although I thought you would be fine."

"Well, I also thought so, but it's good to get the results. This did get me thinking about how my life has gone. I'm divorced and my kids are not doing well. Maybe I have been too focused on my career."

"What are you talking about? You're doing fine. You can't blame yourself for your divorce or your kids' problems. That's out of your control. You had to get out of your marriage. Your ex was very unreasonable, and your kids need to adjust to things. That's just part of life."

"I'm not so sure about all that."

"Look, your life is going well, and things will be back to normal once you're back here in LA."

"Well, maybe you're right. When I was in LA, life seemed to be going well."

"I am right. Just focus on getting well and coming back here."

"I'll try to do that."

"Great, I love you and get some rest."

"Love you too," Chris said as he ended the call and still wondered if things could be different.

TWENTY-SIX

Chris decided to go into the backyard after lunch. Toby followed him out and grabbed the big red ball that was sitting on the porch. He pushed the screen door open ahead of Chris and ran out into the yard. Chris decided to throw a large Frisbee instead that was also on the porch. When he entered the yard from the porch, Toby saw the Frisbee, ran near Chris, and sat on the ground waiting for Chris to throw it. As soon as it left Chris' hand, Toby ran after it.

"At least the dog still likes me. I can't believe how he follows me around all day. I guess he doesn't have any hard feelings about the divorce." Chris smiled to himself as he watched the dog run around the yard.

He remembered mowing the lawn every weekend and catching up with the neighbors on things by stopping to talk with them across the fences along the property lines. In LA, he didn't have a lawn to mow, and he didn't have a clue who his neighbors were. He realized that outside of work, Candace was the only person he talked with at all.

Oddly, he started to miss his old life back in this neighborhood. As he was thinking about this, a voice caught his attention.

"Hey, Chris. How are you doing?" Paul yelled as he was mowing his lawn on a sunny afternoon.

"I'm coming along. I'm not sore from the incisions anymore. In fact, I have hardly used the Vicodin that was prescribed for me when I got home."

"That's great! How's your appetite doing?"

"OK, per my discharge instructions, I can now start trying to resume a normal diet. I've been on a so-called "low residue" diet for the past two weeks; mostly low fiber food. My surgeon told me there is a slight risk of the colon separating from where it was sutured during the first ten days after surgery. I think the odds were 1 in 200. So, one doesn't want to stress the digestion tract much with hard to digest foods or extreme gas!"

"That seems like a good idea to me. Well, it sounds like you are out of the danger zone. Would this be a good time to invite you and your family over for a barbeque this Saturday around 4 pm?"

"I could use some real food. Although I may be a little careful what I eat. That sounds like a great idea. I'll check with Elizabeth at dinner tonight. Thanks for the invite."

"No problem. Let me know if you can make it."

"Will do."

"It seems like almost yesterday when my family moved here," Chris remembered. "In fact, I think I met Paul while mowing my lawn." Chris started to think back to that first meeting.

"Hi, I'm Paul Chambers, and it looks like I'm your new neighbor."

"I'm Chris Baldwin. My wife, Elizabeth, and our three

kids are in the house unpacking boxes. We're from the Chicago area. With the kids getting older, we decided we needed more room. This is a great neighborhood with a train stop for going downtown."

"What grades are your kids in?"

"John is in middle school; Sarah is in grade school, and Jennifer is in pre-school."

"I also work downtown, in the Loop. The train really beats driving in all the traffic and paying the high costs of parking. My wife, Linda, and I have two kids, Michael and Jessica. They're in the same age range as your two older kids. What do you do for a living?"

"I'm a director for business development. I travel some so my wife tends to take care of the home front while I'm away."

"I used to travel a lot in my old job," Paul shared. "After a while I missed not seeing the kids growing up."

"Well, I keep in touch on the phone, and Elizabeth attends most of the events. My kids understand I need to travel in my job so they can live in a nice house in a nice neighborhood like this."

"You're right about the neighborhood," Paul agreed. "There are lots of kids here so they should make some new friends soon. In fact, why don't you and your family join us for a barbeque next Saturday evening? Linda and I can get to know you and Elizabeth while the kids can also meet each other."

"That's very generous of you. I'll let the gang know we have plans for next Saturday. It was great talking with you."

"Same here; and I'll see you next week," Paul said as he started up his mower to finish mowing the backyard.

Chris looked around the yard and wondered where all the years had gone. The kids were getting older, and life had changed so much. He never thought he and Elizabeth would get divorced. They had their problems, but there was a time when they could work them out. As the years went by, it seemed they both got more self-centered and not willing to compromise.

He remembered his father-in-law's advice given as part of his toast at their wedding. He said the key to a good marriage is commitment and compromise. It appeared that both disappeared between him and Elizabeth over the years.

TWENTY-SEVEN

Chris decided to spend the afternoon sitting on the back porch and reading a book. Elizabeth arrived home late in the afternoon. Chris had fallen asleep and awoke when he heard her in the house. She saw him on the porch and decided to join him before getting dinner going.

The porch was enclosed by screens with a few chairs and a table. Elizabeth sat in a chair and looked around the yard for a while before saying a word.

"How was your day?" she finally asked while she was looking out in the backyard.

"It went well. Being at home all day makes me think about what retirement might be like. I don't think I could just stay at home and watch television or read all day."

"Well, you're only stuck in the house a few more weeks. Then you can get back to Los Angeles to be at your job again," Elizabeth replied, careful not to mention he would be back with Candace. She really wasn't in the mood to get into an argument.

"I guess you're right. I should try to enjoy this time off and not complain too much." Chris was relieved she did not mention Candace.

"By the way, Paul Chambers invited us all over to his place for a barbeque this Saturday at four. I told him I'd check with you about it," Chris told Elizabeth.

"That sounds great. I don't know the last time I was at their home. In fact, I don't think I talk with any of my neighbors much anymore. Between work, home, and the kids, I really don't have much time. I kind of miss not seeing Paul and Linda around like we used to. Speaking of dinner, I need to get going on it."

"Do you need some help? I seem to have time available."

"Not really, but I would appreciate the company. I usually get dinner together with no one around," Elizabeth said with a pleasantly surprised look, thinking how alone she really was at times.

While she prepared the food, Elizabeth told Chris about her day at work and caught up on what it had been like there over the past couple of years. Chris talked about his job, carefully avoiding any mention of Candace. For the moment, the two of them forgot about their differences and just enjoyed being together and talking about ordinary things.

Linda yelled up the stairwell, telling her kids that dinner was ready. For once everyone was home but in their own rooms. She thought that they should interact more with each other than just sit in their rooms watching TV or playing video games.

"Give me a few more minutes, I'm busy right now," Sarah yelled back, as she was on her cell phone talking about going out with her friends that weekend and meeting up with some guys at the mall.

"I'll be down soon," John shouted down as he was trying to make the next level in his video game.

Jennifer didn't reply at all since she was absorbed in a television series.

"Let's go or your father and I will start without you, and the last one down will clean up after dinner," Linda threatened.

Suddenly all three were running down the stairs and towards the dining room. They sat down and started to pass the food around when Jennifer suggested they say grace before eating.

"We never say grace before dinner," John protested, anxious just to eat dinner.

"Now maybe we should think about doing this, at least this time," Elizabeth said softly as she tried to head off an argument.

"I'll agree to anything just to get started eating dinner," Sarah added.

"OK, Jennifer, you can go ahead," Chris said, not sure how to respond to her suggestion.

After an awkward moment of silence, Jennifer thanked God for the food before them and for having the whole family together for dinner. Chris and Elizabeth looked at each other briefly and smiled at each other.

At dinner that evening, Chris told his children their plans to visit the Chambers at the weekend.

"I really don't want to go there on Saturday," John quickly spoke up almost before Chris finished his comments.

"Do you have other plans?" Christopher asked.

"No. I just don't like his kids, especially Michael. He's such a nerd."

"How's that?"

"For one thing, he hangs out with the smart kids at school. And he and his sister talk about their church youth group with me sometimes. They even invited me to go."

"What did you think about that?"

"Are you crazy? No one who is cool would go to a youth group. I bet they sit around and talk about how they're better than the rest of us."

"That's not so. We do lots of fun stuff," interjected Jennifer. "We also talk about how God is always with us, no matter what problems we're dealing with."

"Well, I think Michael is kind of cute, so I'm OK with going," added Sarah.

"So, it's settled. The ayes have it four to one," Elizabeth declared, trying to end the conversation.

"I didn't know this was up for a vote," John protested.

"Look, it's only for a few hours. Besides, if I remember right, Paul barbeques chicken like no one else I know," Christopher replied, slyly trying to avoid a confrontation. "Also, it will be nice for all of us to do something together."

"Well, I'm not sure about the togetherness stuff, but you sold me on the chicken," John said to the relief of both Christopher and Elizabeth.

After dinner, Chris and Elizabeth talked about the upcoming weekend while they cleaned up.

"It will be nice to get together with the Chambers. I remember how we did this regularly when the kids were younger," Elizabeth reminded Chris.

"It seems a long time ago now. Paul and Linda always seem to have things together with their lives and their kids. Maybe we had been too focused on our own careers and ourselves and not paying enough attention to the family and each other," Chris said while he looked out the window into the backyard.

"Well, what's done is done, and we can only look towards

the future. I think it will be a good starting point getting together with Paul and Linda. At least we can pretend things are back to the way they used to be for an evening."

"I agree with that," Chris said as they finished picking up after dinner.

Afterwards Elizabeth called Linda about the weekend plans.

"Hi Linda, it's Elizabeth. Chris told me about your generous invitation for this weekend. We are all looking forward to it. I admit we had to bribe John with the promise of Paul's barbeque chicken!"

"That's fine. Paul will consider it a compliment. He learned how to barbecue chicken when he was in Texas for a month on a business trip when we lived in Seattle, and he worked for Boeing. That seems so long ago now."

"A lot of things seem like a long time ago. Thanks again for the invite, and we look forward to seeing you on Saturday. Oh, is there anything I can bring?"

"No, thanks. We're just looking forward to having a nice evening with you and your family."

"Me too," Elizabeth said as she ended the call and thought back to the days before her divorce.

TWENTY-EIGHT

A couple of days later, Jennifer talked with Jessica at lunch in school.

"I'm glad we could get together for lunch today. I wanted to talk with you about my family coming over to your house this Saturday for a barbeque," Jennifer said to Jessica as they found a corner table to sit and talk without being bothered with too much noise in the school cafeteria.

"Yes, I'm kind of excited to have you and your whole family over at the house. I can't remember the last time your family and mine got together."

"Probably before my parents got divorced. That was a long time ago! I guess what you mean by my 'whole' family is my mom, brother, sister, and my dad."

"Now that you mention it, I hadn't thought of it that way. That is including your dad, but I guess that is your whole family."

"My mom told us that's why my dad is staying with us. She said even though they're divorced, he's still part of the family. I hadn't really thought of it that way for a long time. After he moved out of the house and got divorced from my mom, he used to visit us regularly, and we would stay at his apartment sometimes. We had a regular schedule for visits, which was kind of weird, but I got used to it and enjoyed seeing him. After he moved to LA, he didn't call much, and I haven't seen him until now. So, I guess I didn't think of him as part of my family in the usual way for a while."

"I don't know how I would handle it if my parents got divorced. I heard your dad had surgery and is staying at your house to recover," Jessica said with concern.

"Yea, he had a polyp removed along with part of his colon, and he needs to stay here for six weeks to rest."

"That sounds like a nasty operation! How's he doing?"

"He seems to be doing OK. He just sits around all day watching sports or news channels on TV. He plays with Toby in the yard some too. I think he misses the dog more than us," Jennifer said with a sigh.

"I'm sure that's not true. He probably feels strange being back here after so long," Jessica quickly replied.

"You may be right. I also feel kind of weird having him around all the time. I sort of got used to him not being here. Just mom and us."

"How's your mom handling it? Have they been arguing with each other?"

"No, they seem to be doing OK. I know my mom is still very upset about the divorce. It doesn't help that my dad is dating someone that is about 25 years old."

"Wow, she could be your older sister! Think of that."

"Now that's a creepy thought. Thanks for putting that thought into my head!" Jennifer laughed about it, thinking it was a funny idea.

"I remember when we used to all play together when we were little."

"Yea, now only you and I still hang out together. John and Sarah have new friends, but my mom doesn't approve of them. Especially John's friends. They party a lot and get drunk sometimes. I hear him coming home late at night, even on school nights. I think he may have tried drugs but not sure," Jessica said softly so no one overheard.

"What does your mom do about it?"

"Not much. She has tried to talk with him and even get counseling, but he's not interested. He said it's no big deal, and everyone in high school parties and drinks beer."

"My brother Michael told me kids in high school do that. He said he gets hassled by them for not partying and drinking. I know some kids in our junior high school also drink and smoke cigarettes, and some also do drugs."

"Why do they do this? I don't see how that makes them happy."

"I think they want to fit in with the cool kids. Let's face it, we aren't considered cool kids to hang out with," Jessica said with a bit of sarcasm. "If that's what it takes to be cool, I don't want to be a part of it."

"That reminds me of a joke I heard about drugs: 'Reality is for people who can't handle drugs,'" Jennifer said to her as they both laughed.

"Hey, I want to tell you that John was not that interested in going to your house for the barbeque. I shouldn't tell you this, but he said your brother Michael was a nerd because he doesn't hang out with the cool kids."

"That won't be a news item for Michael, but I won't tell him. To be honest, your brother is one of the kids Michael talks about. I can't believe they used to be good friends. They used to play sports together and hang out at our houses after school."

"I think my parents' problems got to him, and he was looking for an escape from reality. His so-called 'friends' help him do that with alcohol and drugs. I think your brother is cool. In fact, here's another thing I shouldn't tell you. My sister Sarah said she thought he was kind of cute. She had no problem going to your house."

"So why is John coming over?"

"My mom told him about your dad's great barbeque chicken. It looks like food got his interest."

"There will be someone else at the barbeque that might interest John besides my father's awesome chicken. Emma Clark will be there. As you know, she's in our youth group and maybe she can have a positive influence on John without him knowing it," Jessica said with a hint of secrecy in her voice and a smile.

"So, does Sarah like high school?" Jessica asked as she thought about her comments about John.

"My mom thought she was also hanging out with the wrong kids. Her friends are getting into dating and partying. I think she wants to be accepted, and this is one way of doing that. I think it's also due to the divorce. She never said much about it, but I think it really bothered her a lot. Maybe this is how she's dealing with it."

"She always had friends in our school. I don't think she needs to look for new ones in high school. Maybe Michael can also have a good influence on Sarah. You know God works through people to help others."

"So, you're saying maybe God may use Emma and Michael to help my brother and sister without them knowing it?"

"Something like that," Jessica replied with a smile.

"You know, I'm glad you invited me to your youth group

a couple of years ago. I really felt bad about my parents' divorce and even wondered if it was my fault."

"Hey, I just thought you could use some more friends and a safe place to talk about your feelings. There are a lot of kids with the same problems you had. Also, our youth pastor is very easy to talk with and seems to know what kids are going through."

"Anyway, the group and your pastor really got me through some tough stuff. I hope I can use what I learned at home to help my family. They don't talk a lot about things, but I think they all could use some help. Just getting together this weekend with your family feels like a step towards getting back to normal."

"I'll keep you and your family in my prayers. We better get going before we're late for class," Jessica said as they got up to leave.

TWENTY-NINE

On Saturday, the family all got ready to head over to the Chambers house.

"Come on, we need to get going!" Elizabeth yelled up the spiral staircase as she was waiting for John, Sarah, and Jessica to get ready to leave.

"We're coming," Jennifer shouted as she was waiting for Sarah to get out of the hall bathroom.

"What's taking you so long in there?" Jennifer banged on the bathroom door.

"She wants to look really nice for Michael," John teased as he went by them and headed down the stairs.

"Is that true?" Jennifer teased Sarah.

"No, I was just getting my teeth brushed," she said tersely as she opened the door and headed downstairs.

Finally, the family gathered in the foyer before leaving.

"Is everyone here?" Chris asked as he did a headcount reminiscent of when the children were little. "OK, everyone is accounted for. Let's go!" he said jokingly.

Toby wanted to accompany them too, thinking they were going on a walk. He was not used to seeing them leave through the front door unless he went with them for a walk.

The group headed out the front door and walked to the Chambers' home next door. The house was similar to their home, which was typical for the neighborhood.

"Hey Linda, it's great to see you again," Chris said as she opened the door wide.

"Paul told me you're feeling better."

"Yes, I am. I think I'm ready to eat some real food but with caution."

"Thanks again for inviting us," Elizabeth added.

"No problem; I see you have all the kids here. Why don't you guys go out into the backyard and say hi to Michael and Jessica?"

"It's been a while since we've seen you and Chris," Linda said as they sat down in the living room to talk. "Although it hasn't been the best of circumstances, it is nice to see you both again. The neighborhood is not the same without you."

"I'm sure the neighborhood is getting along fine without me," Chris said sarcastically.

"Well, we miss not seeing you around. So, what have you been up to?"

"My job in LA had been going well up until I needed this surgery. Now, who knows what will happen. They have some guy I don't know handling my clients and going off to Europe to close a major deal. If I were there, that deal would pretty much seal up my promotion to executive vice president. Now, who knows if I'll even be considered for the position! My boss tried to get me to defer my surgery until after the trip to Europe."

"Did I ever tell you how we ended up here and with my consulting firm?" Paul asked Chris, thinking this may be a good moment to provide some perspective on his job situation.

"Now that you mention it, I don't recall," Chris replied.

"When we lived in Seattle and I was at Boeing, I worked my way up to being Technical Director for new products. I oversaw all engineering work done on a new airplane with all sorts of chief engineers reporting to me along with some program managers. I did some travel to visit customers to get their input on product development. Having a PhD in engineering, I really enjoyed this work, getting involved in all sorts of technical details and solving challenging problems. I also enjoyed mentoring young engineers new to the company and just out of college.

"Things were going along well there, and the kids were growing up faster than I could imagine. Linda, being a teacher, had always been helpful. She kept the same schedule as the kids so she could get them to practice or attend most games or school events, while I may miss a few with travel. I got to most events though.

"Then one day I was asked if I would be interested in taking over the program management oversight for new products. This would mean moving to Chicago. It also meant a big increase in salary along with much more travel. After thinking about it for a while and talking with the family, I decided to accept the job. With the promotion, we could live in a much larger home and take very nice vacations. The downside was I was not home three out of four weeks a month, traveling to see customers. I did enjoy getting this 'big picture' view of the company, but I realized I was losing touch with my family. I missed most games and school events. I also missed the technical work and mentoring young engineers."

"Well, didn't Linda cover for you while you were away? I think your primary job was providing for your family, even if that means being away some," Chris said confused when Paul paused for a moment.

"That is what I thought too. After a while, I started thinking how much I was missing, and phone calls to home from hotels were not enough. I needed to have face to face time with Linda and the kids. I discussed the idea of leaving Boeing and starting my own consulting company in Chicago.

"I think the Holy Spirit was moving me in this direction because after I mentioned this idea to my boss, he said Boeing had been thinking about outsourcing some work to an outside firm, and my proposed company would be a great fit. So, I started Chicago Engineering Associates, LLC. I also started teaching in the evenings at Northwestern University so I could mentor engineering students with the time I had from not traveling very much. Of course, I also could keep up with the kids' activities and even sneak out of work early for a soccer or lacrosse practice!" Paul said, as he finished his story.

"That's a great story, but I don't think I have the same options," Chris responded. "By the way, what do you mean about the 'Holy Spirit' moving you to start your company?"

"The Holy Spirit is God telling us what to do. Although, I admit I don't always know if I'm doing what He wants me to do."

"Now you're sounding like Pastor Jim," Chris replied, not wanting to get more into a discussion on God.

"I will take that as a compliment," Paul said with a smile. "Also, the point of my story is that sometimes there are things more important than work or money. I've been reminded of this over the years when I see people retire after spending decades becoming experts in their field and just walk away, and we never hear from them again. I just wondered, although we spend eight hours plus travel for work five days a week, how important is it in our lives? We need to make a living, but do we work to live or live to work? So, I think work many times gets a very high priority in people's lives without them realizing how unimportant it is to them compared to other aspects of their lives such as family or other activities."

"I never thought of it that way. I can also think of people who retired, and we never hear from them again," Chris said as he started to reconsider his own decisions over the years about his job and Elizabeth.

"We can continue this conversation outside while I start the grill," Paul suggested.

"That sounds like a good idea. I'm getting hungry. I haven't had that feeling since my surgery," Chris replied as they both got up and headed for the yard.

THIRTY

So how are things with you?" Linda asked Elizabeth after Paul and Chris left to start the barbeque.

"Pretty hectic. My job keeps me busy, and I barely get home in time to get dinner going and catch up with what my kids have been doing. I have to admit, I get a bit overwhelmed at times, and the children notice it."

"I had that same feeling when Paul traveled a lot. It must be very difficult to handle work and children by yourself."

"It's been very tough. I don't share much of this with Chris. I've known you for a long time and consider you a good friend, so I feel comfortable sharing some of my difficulties with you. Although Chris and I fought a lot while we were married, at least I had some help at home. Paul's story reminded me of Chris and me—both putting our careers first and us and the children second or third. I used to go on trips a lot or Chris would go when I was home. Also, he expected me to cover things at home if he had to work late or travel."

"Paul and I didn't know what to say or do when you and Chris separated and then divorced. How are the kids doing?"

"Not very well. Jennifer appears to be doing the best in the group. She and Jessica get along well, and I appreciate the good influence she has had on Jennifer. I'm not sure about why she has gotten so involved in your church, but I am happy she has found a good group of friends."

"I believe God uses people to do His will. Perhaps, He is working through Jessica to help Jennifer. This is what Paul was talking about with the Holy Spirit influencing him about what he should do with his job.

"I never thought about this, although I kind of remember hearing about it when I was a kid in my parents' church. Our family has never been much for going to church except for Christmas and Easter."

"You're always welcome to join us to attend a weekend service anytime."

"Thanks. After seeing how Jennifer has been influenced by your church, I will consider it."

"I've kept you and your family in my prayers since you told me that you and Chris were separating a few years ago."

"I don't know what to make of prayer. I remember the pastor in the church I grew up in always talking about the power of prayer. I prayed for things, and nothing happened."

"It might have been you were praying for things that God knew better than to grant."

"Now that you mention it, most were self-centered prayers. So, what do you think about prayer?"

"I really believe that God listens to all prayers. Even Jesus talked to God, His Father, through prayer. He prayed many times before performing miracles like feeding thousands of people that were following Him or raising His friend Lazarus from the dead."

"So, you're saying anything is possible with prayer."

"That's exactly what I'm saying. Did you ever ask God to

help you when your marriage was starting to have problems?"

"No, I didn't even think about praying. Besides, it's too late to pray about it now."

"That depends on you."

"What do you mean by that?"

"Look, this is getting personal, but we've been friends for a long time, and I feel I need to ask you this. Do you still care about Chris, and the marriage you had with him?" Linda asked cautiously, not sure of the response she would get.

"What we had seems so long ago, and so much has happened since our divorce.

"Ignoring all that, do you still care about your relationship with Chris?"

"When he called about staying here for six weeks after having surgery, I was so mad, and I told him all kinds of things. But, after settling down, I asked him if he had cancer, and I was relieved to hear the polyps appeared benign. I'm not sure he caught that in the sound of my voice. So, yes, and deep down maybe I still care about the marriage we had and, in some way, wonder if that could happen again," Elizabeth said with exasperation.

"Wow, so maybe there is a reason for Chris being here! God may have used the circumstances for a second chance for your marriage," Linda said excitedly.

"How do you think that?" Elizabeth questioned her.

"There are many stories in the Bible where God uses people in situations for a greater good than they even realize at the time," Linda began. "One famous story is about Joseph, left for dead by his brothers in the desert. He's taken to Egypt as a servant but eventually becomes second in command of Egypt after Pharaoh and saves them from starvation during a long draught. He also reconciles with his family."

"You're telling me, apart from the famine and being left for dead, Chris being here may be like Joseph being in Egypt?" Elizabeth asked with a sarcastic laugh.

"Something like that."

"I got to admit, this whole thing seems a little strange."

"Let's pray together about this," Linda suggested after a long pause.

"I'm not sure about this praying stuff. Like I said, I haven't seen it work in the past."

"Well, you need to trust God to take control of your life and not try to control everything yourself."

"I'm feeling like I don't have control of my kids, my job, or my life right now, so maybe it's time to ask God for help. Even though I've always believed in Him, I haven't done much with it."

"Maybe it's time to start. Like I said, it's never too late for God to step in and intervene. Let's pray."

In the middle of the living room, the two women sat forward in their chairs, and Linda led them in prayer.

"Lord, you know all our needs before coming to You about them. We're asking You to step in and heal the broken relationship between Chris and Elizabeth. Help them to see things the way they were when they first were in love with each other. Open their hearts and minds to Your will for them. Let the Holy Spirit work in them to reveal Your plan for their lives. This will not be an easy path but with Your help, they can do what looks impossible for us but is possible for You. In Jesus" name, we pray. Amen."

Elizabeth started to sob quietly as Linda finished the prayer.

"I can't believe how your prayer affected me. It's like all

sorts of emotions that I kept deep inside me were let loose," Elizabeth said as she stopped sobbing and dried her eyes. "I can't let Chris, or the kids see me like this."

"Why don't you go to the hall bath and wash your face and settle down. If you like, we can meet again another day to talk about how God can fix any problem."

"Before today, I wouldn't have even considered talking about how God can help me and Chris, but now I think I'm open to that discussion."

"Great! You go get cleaned up, and I better check on how dinner is going."

"Paul, inside the house you talked about the Holy Spirit. I'm not sure what that is all about," Chris asked while Paul was getting the chicken on the grill.

"Like I said, it's God speaking to us. It's also like Jesus talking to us. The three are one. You may remember hearing about the Father, Son, and Holy Spirit being one. Jesus told the apostles that the Holy Spirit would come to advise them after He was raised from the dead," Paul explained.

"So how do you hear the Spirit talking to you?"

"Sometimes in prayer I will hear it, or if I try to be still or quiet and just wait. I don't always hear it, and I'm not sure when I do at times."

"Do you pray a lot?"

"I try to read some passages from the Bible and pray every day, if possible. I do miss doing this sometimes. When I don't do this, I feel like I'm missing something. I connect with God during those devotional times."

"I never thought about connecting personally with God. He has always seemed to be far away."

"That's where the Holy Spirit comes in. I believe every

Christian has the Holy Spirit living within them, so God and Jesus are always present."

"How does reading the Bible and praying help you? What do you pray about?"

"All kinds of things, including you and your family."

"Really, you pray for us?"

"Sure, I know things have been very difficult, and prayer can help."

"Well, I appreciate it, but I don't think prayer will fix all the problems Elizabeth and I have with the kids."

"I believe all things are possible for God, including helping in your situation."

"How did you get so involved in church and God?" Chris asked, seeing a different side of Paul he had never seen before.

"Back in Seattle, some friends of ours invited us to their church. I wasn't sure about going. I had drifted away from the church as I got older, but the message from the pastor caught my attention. He talked about how since the beginning of time God wanted us to be in relationship with Him.

"Over time I saw this in the stories in the Old Testament, and then Jesus talks about God being our heavenly Father. It seemed to make sense, and I started to read the Bible every day. I even tried praying. I found passages in the Bible sometimes talked to me about something I was dealing with at that moment, which really shocked me at first. Praying helped me focus on letting God take control instead of me. That was a freeing experience for me. I didn't worry as much about every detail of my life."

"You have a Ph.D. in engineering. I wouldn't expect someone with an analytical perspective to be that committed to something we can't see," Chris said with surprise.

"As a part of studying the scriptures and talking with other Christians, I discovered how Jesus fulfills all prophesies made about Him in the Old Testament. In addition, I figure if His resurrection from the dead did not happen, it would not still be talked about today."

"Why do you think that?"

"There were so many witnesses that saw Him after He rose from the dead. Why would that many people lie about something like that? No other religious leader has ever come back from the dead. So, Jesus is the one and only Son of God. He died for all our sins so we can be made right before God. I would like to sum it up this way: 'Jesus left his divinity, became human, and died for all our sins.'"

"Wow, this really impacted you!" Chris exclaimed, trying to get his mind around all he had just heard.

"It really did. Maybe you can think about what we've been talking about. Feel free to talk with me about it again when you're ready."

"I might do that. Nothing else has been working for me, so reading some scriptures may not be a bad idea."

THIRTY-ONE

What do you think about this chicken?" Paul asked as he went over to the grill to check the meat.

"It looks and smells great. I'll need to watch how much I eat. I get some digestion problems if I eat too much."

"Well, I won't be insulted if you leave food on your plate!" Paul joked with a grin as they sat down on lawn chairs and watched the grill.

"Hi, Jennifer," Jessica said as Sarah and her siblings went into the backyard. "Hey, John and Sarah, I haven't seen you guys for a while."

"I guess that's because we're in high school, and you and my little sister are in junior high school," Sarah teased.

"Hi, Michael," Sarah said as she hoped to get his attention. "What have you been doing lately?"

"Not much. There's someone here I want you to meet. This is Emma Clark," Michael told the group.

"I don't think I've seen you around the high school," John said, trying to hide his immediate attraction to her.

"That's because I don't go to your high school," Emma explained. "I live in the next town but attend Michael's church and youth group. I'm new to the area, and he invited me here to meet you guys and maybe begin to get to know you."

"I'd be glad to show you around the area sometime," John volunteered quickly.

"That's great. I may take you up on it. I don't think I've seen you at our youth group meetings or outings," Emma added.

"No, I'm not a member," John said slowly, not sure how to reply.

"You don't need to be a member of the church. We have lots of kids who just go to the youth group. Hey, why don't you and Sarah stop by at our next meeting? We're planning a camping trip to Michigan."

"That sounds like it might be fun," John replied, not sure what he might have been getting into, but he was sure he would like to get to know Emma better.

"Yea, we do a lot of fun things," Jennifer added.

"I thought you just went to church and talked about God and stuff like that," Sarah said to Michael and Emma.

"I know a lot of kids think that. I guess everyone has stereotypes. In addition to doing fun things, we do talk about God and our relationship with him and Jesus."

"So, how is that interesting to do?" John asked skeptically. "It seems like it would get really boring, kind of like school."

"Why do you find school boring? I like most of my classes plus I'm on the soccer team. The guys on the team are great," Mchael replied.

"It's like what are we going to do with this stuff they teach us in school?"

"Well, I'm not sure what I want to do for a job. My dad is trying to get me interested in engineering, but I'm thinking of business or law."

"My dad is bugging me about what I want to do after high school."

"He sounds like my father. I think they just want the best for us."

"At least your dad is living at your house. Our father decided to leave and move to LA for a job and now is dating what I think is a hot girlfriend."

"That must be hard. I don't know how I'd be if my parents got divorced," Michael said sympathetically.

"It really sucks," Sarah added.

"Have you talked with them about how you feel?"

"Why bother? They're too busy with their own problems," Sarah replied.

"You may be surprised. Just try to talk with them and see what happens."

"Maybe you're right. It can't get any worse than it is now."

"So, do you play any sports?" Michael asked John.

"No. I used to play baseball, but I didn't want to put all the time into practice for the high school team. I did try out, and the coach said he thought I was pretty good. He tried to get me to join the team, but I wasn't interested."

"So, Sarah, do you have any interests outside of school?" Emma asked.

"I do like shopping at the mall with friends, but I don't play any sports, like Jennifer plays Lacrosse."

"I also like shopping. Maybe we can get together sometime?" Emma offered.

"Sure, that would be great!"

"So, when are you guys meeting about the camping trip?" John asked to keep the conversation going with Emma.

"Next Friday night. If you like, you, Sarah, and Jennifer

can come with Jessica and me. My mom has plenty of room in the van."

"That sounds great!" John said quickly. "What do you think, Sarah?"

"I don't know. Maybe, I'll see if my friends have anything planned," Sarah replied, thinking it may be a good opportunity to get to know Michael, but she didn't want to seem as eager as John was, making himself so obviously interested in Emma. *That's just the way boys are,* she thought.

"You can invite them too," Emma interjected.

"Thanks, but I really don't see them going to a church youth group meeting," Sarah replied, quickly hoping her friends didn't hear that she went to a youth group meeting. She would be banished from the inner circle of friends forever!

"Is everyone ready for some food?" Paul asked as everyone began gathering around the patio with the installed grill and benches nearby.

"No problem. It's just great for all of us to get together," Paul quickly replied.

"This reminds me of the many summer weekends we used to get together," Paul continued after everyone settled down to eat. "John, what are you thinking about doing after high school? I know next year is your senior year."

"My dad wants me to go to college, but I'm not sure that's right for me."

"Well, it is a big decision. I think people are most successful and happy with their careers if they're doing something they really want to do. Most people probably don't have those kinds of jobs. That's partly why I left my old job and started my own consulting firm. I wasn't doing what I really enjoyed doing. So, what do you really enjoy doing?"

"That's a hard question. I don't know what I really like to do."

"I have a suggestion if it's OK with your parents. Would you consider spending some time at my consulting firm this summer as an intern? This would give you an idea of what engineers do."

"I'm not sure I'm interested in engineering. I don't even like my math and science classes. They don't seem very relevant."

"That may change after you see what engineers do with those subjects. We have some interesting projects. Right now, one of them is reviewing a design for a large office building that will be constructed in downtown Chicago."

"I do like my art classes and my teacher said that architects bring art to buildings and homes they design," John said.

"Well, this may be a chance for you to think about architecture as a career. As your teacher said, they create designs, and engineers like me will make sure they won't collapse!" Paul said, happy that he sparked some interest in John.

Elizabeth had shared her concerns about him with Linda, and Paul saw an opportunity to maybe help. "Actually, architects also need to take some math and engineering classes so they have an idea of what designs will be stable before an engineer takes a closer look at it."

"That works for me," Chris said, as he affirmed Paul's invitation to John.

"Me too," Elizabeth said as she tried not to reveal her total surprise that John would be interested at all.

"That sounds interesting, but I don't think there are many women in engineering," Sarah added.

"You're right, there being more men than women in the

field, but the number of women is growing. In fact, my senior partner is a woman, Dr. Rebecca Evans. She was the first person to join my company. If you're interested, I can arrange for you to meet her. She's always interested in talking with girls about careers in science and engineering. She also has some funny stories about sometimes being the only women in a class in college."

"Even in high school, it seems like there are all these nerdy guys in the AP science and math classes and not a lot of girls. It might be fun to talk about this stuff," Sarah said and then added, "Maybe we could get lunch and go shopping along Michigan Avenue after our discussion?"

"I think she would be open to that suggestion."

"Both John and Sarah are interested in our camping trip and are coming to the youth group meeting next Friday night," Jennifer told the group.

"That's great!" Linda said. "The kids always have a great time on those trips. It's nice to get away from the city for a few days."

"Jennifer and I had a great time last year," Jennifer shared. "I really enjoyed being around the campfire at night and seeing all the stars. Pastor Jim is an amateur astronomer and showed us the constellations. He even brought his telescope for us to view some planets and other neat stuff."

"Hey, it's getting late, and we better get back to the house," Elizabeth announced. "Thanks so much for a wonderful evening. It was a great time."

"I agree. It was nice getting both families together again," Linda said as she and Paul walked with the Baldwin family through the house and to the front door.

THIRTY-TWO

That was a fun time at Paul and Linda's place," Elizabeth told Chris as they were sitting in the living room. The kids had already gone back to their bedrooms, as usual.

"I agree. While we were there, I started thinking back to the old days—the kids playing with Michael and Jessica, along with other kids in the neighborhood. I remember when we moved here, they invited us over for a barbeque, and we all got to know each other. I guess their barbeque tradition carries on, even now."

"I was starting to think about Paul's comments about work not defining people. He said how when people retired, no one heard from them again in the workplace," Elizabeth told him. "I was thinking about us. Were we so wrapped up with our careers that we forgot about taking care of each other or even paying enough attention to the kids?" Elizabeth asked.

"I don't know. Why do we spend so much time in college and graduate school if our careers aren't important? Paul has a PhD in engineering and seems to have done well, even though he said his work is not as important as it used to be."

"Well, he adjusted. I know from talking with Linda over the years, they had a lot of discussions about his time away from home. I think their involvement in church also influenced them, especially Paul," she replied.

"There it goes back to that church thing again. I really don't understand it. Even in LA, I know people that talk about Jesus and God and how it has changed their lives. However, I also know some self-proclaimed Christians who don't behave any different than the rest of us and maybe worse. One Christian manager I know in marketing will say anything to close a deal. I wonder what Jesus would say about that?"

"I know what you mean. I'm aware of several divorced families that attend church regularly. So, what's the difference?" Elizabeth asked.

"I really don't know. In a lot of ways, I don't see any difference in the way Christians behave and the rest of us. So why should I think about becoming a Christian when I see no difference between them and me?" Chris replied with a curious tone in his voice.

"Linda and I prayed for our family today after you and Paul went outside to start the grill," Elizabeth said with a little hesitancy in her voice, not sure if she should tell Chris.

"Why did you do that?" Chris asked with total surprise in his voice.

"Linda started to talk about her faith and the power of prayer. She then just offered to pray for us. I was just overwhelmed. I don't remember anyone offering to pray for me."

"What did she pray for?"

"She prayed that God would help us work out our problems."

"It seems too late for that."

"She said it's never too late for God to help."

"Paul was telling me about the Holy Spirit being in all

Christians. I'm not sure it is living in me, and I'm not sure I would consider myself a Christian. I also am not so sure God listens to our prayers. So, do you think your praying with Linda will help work out some of our problems with our kids?"

"Who knows? I will say this: Lakeside Community Church has had a positive influence on Jennifer, and maybe it will have one on the other two kids. I was surprised to hear they were interested in the youth group camping trip."

"I agree. I'm not sure what's up with that. So, back to the career discussion; should we have been more compromising?" Chris asked.

"I don't know. Who would compromise, you or me?" Elizabeth asked.

"Good question. That was probably partly why we got divorced; we could never compromise on anything," Chris said.

"So, are you happier being divorced and not compromising, or would you be happier married and compromising?" Elizabeth asked.

"There was a time I would have said getting divorced was the only option available," Chris responded.

"And now?"

"Since I've been back here, I'm not so sure," Chris said as he looked straight into Elizabeth's eyes. They both realized they hadn't looked each other directly in the eyes in a very long time.

After a prolonged moment, Elizabeth abruptly commented that it was getting late, and she was very tired.

After she left for her bedroom, Chris thought back to their early days together and how they would take long walks in the neighborhood and talk about the future. Everything seemed so perfect then. They would be the perfect couple with perfect kids. They had their whole lives planned out like a script. They never thought about anything coming between them and their plans, especially themselves.

Then he thought about how life changed after the kids were born and got older. Life had gotten complicated. He remembered one particular incident:

"Chris, we need to talk," Elizabeth said after dinner when the kids had left the dining room, and they were cleaning the dishes in the kitchen.

"Sure, what's up?"

"I need more help around the house and with the kids."

"I told you that getting a job was a bad idea. We don't need the money, and my job keeps me away some with long hours and travel."

"We talked about all this when I was thinking about getting back to work. Now with the kids in school, I have a lot of time on my hands, and I miss the adult company all day, like it was when I worked before we had kids."

"We had agreed that you would quit your job and stay at home once we started a family. You would focus on the children and I on my job. Maybe you could volunteer at the schools. I think they're always looking for people."

"I do some of that already, but I feel like I want to get back into the workplace. You remember I have a marketing degree from Harvard?"

"Yes, I do, and if I recall right, that's where I met you," Chris said, trying to lighten up the conversation as he hugged her.

"Nice try, but I really need more help at home. Sometimes I need to stay late at work, and I get behind on everything at home."

"You know I can't just drop everything to head home either. This is what makes two parents working very difficult."

"It is even worse when you must travel for business. I knew I couldn't have a job that involved travel, so I limited my options to make it work. Now I'm not so sure."

"If it's getting too hard to keep your job and handle things at home, just quit your job."

"I can't do that, and I won't do that. I enjoy getting out of the house each day. Also, this job helps me keep my skills current to be ready for a better job once the kids are older."

"What do you mean by that?" Chris was confused.

"I want to get back into a career once the kids are more independent. Isn't this what we used to talk about when we were dating? We would have two successful careers and the perfect family."

"I'm not so sure that's possible in the real world of day-to-day life," Chris said as he remembered those days that seem so long ago.

"Well, I do think this is possible. Look, I didn't go to college just to stay at home after the kids were born. I decided to stay at home while they were young because I wanted to be there for their first steps and be there for the first years when so much happens."

"I thought you enjoyed this and now I am hearing something else," Chris said, trying to sort out what she was trying to tell him.

"I do enjoy it, but now I need to do something for myself. I've been doing things for everyone else for years. I need some time for me."

"I'm not sure if this can work out. My job isn't very flexible."

"Is it your job that's not flexible or you? I'm not sure how much effort you make to give home any priority over work."

"Look, I worked very hard for where I am today. My father worked in a shop his whole life and wanted something better for me and my brothers and sisters. My mom got a part time job once we were all in school to help put money away for college. I worked hard in school and did well at UMass. I worked summers to help pay for my tuition and room and board. Again, working hard and giving school my priority. I got a good first job and then got to Harvard Business School. I did all this so I could supply my family with more than I had as a kid."

"So, do you think you were deprived growing up in a working-class family?"

"No, but how would you know anything about that? I grew up in Holyoke while you grew up in Newton."

"I'm not going to apologize to anyone for my family's affluence. However, it wasn't much before their generation when my family also did not have much money," Elizabeth replied, surprised at the unexpected comments about her family. As far as she knew, Chris thought highly of her parents, and this kind of thought had never been mentioned before.

"Well, I wanted to make sure my family didn't have to worry about that either."

"Look, you've been a great provider for all of us. But sometimes we need you and not your money at home. Do you understand that?"

"My dad worked almost every day of the week, and I think I turned out fine."

"He did that because he had to. You don't. Isn't that part of doing better than the earlier generation?" Elizabeth asked.

"So, you want me to work less so you can work more?"

"That's not what I'm saying. What I'm saying is I need some help at home so I can also realize some other dreams. I love being a mom, and our family is great. I just need to do some things that I dreamed about before all of this came about."

"I don't know if I can do what you need done. My work has gotten so complicated; it's hard to pull back. I'm close to really moving up in the company. Giving less priority now will kill any chances for my advancement."

"Will you at least consider spending more time at home and less at work?" Elizabeth asked, completely exasperated with the conversation.

"OK, OK, I'll think about it," Chris replied with agitation in his voice, also tired out from the discussion.

And that's where their discussion had ended. Nothing had been resolved. Chris often wondered if they had missed something vital that could have changed everything.

Chris' cell phone rang and brought him back to the present.

"Hey there, how's it going?" Candace said as he answered a midnight call later that night. It was only nine in the evening in Los Angeles.

"It's going well here. We went over to our old friends Paul and Linda Chambers for a barbeque. I haven't seen them in quite a while. Our families used to get together regularly years ago."

"It sounds like you miss those days," Candace said with annoyance in her voice.

"Look, this was a significant part of my life, and I admit

it was nice reliving it again, if only for a short time."

"Well, is our relationship as significant as that one?" she asked testily.

"Of course, it is. We all have past lives, and there are good and bad parts, I'm sure for everyone."

"I'm beginning to wonder if you going to Chicago was a good idea."

"Remember, I asked you to stay with me, but you had too much business travel."

"I know, but it sounds like you may be having some regrets about leaving Chicago in the first place."

"I may be reminiscing some, but I don't regret going to LA. Also, I wouldn't have met you if I were still in Chicago."

"That's a good point. It's just that I don't like you spending so much time with your ex-wife."

"Look, I have just three weeks left before I'm approved by my surgeon to resume normal activities, and then I can head back to LA."

"I guess I'll survive not seeing you until then. Have you heard much from Sam about how the guy covering for you at work is doing?"

"Sam told me he's doing OK, and he heard him saying he may be in line for the executive vice-president's job that, until my surgery, I had a virtual lock on. I can't do anything about it. I'm just not in control of things right now."

"You had better get back as soon as you can, or you may lose that promotion," Candace said emphatically.

"Like I just said, I can't leave for another three weeks."

"Are you going to let some doctor stand in the way of your promotion? Think of the great trips we could take with that extra cash. We've been thinking of moving in together. Your promotion could help us get a really nice place."

"I might have bent the rules at work from time to time to get things done, but I won't with my health. The last thing I want is to be back in the hospital for more surgery."

"You worry too much. I don't like your whole attitude since you went to Chicago. You also talk more about the past and about your kids. You never talked about your kids before."

"You're right and I should have. Since getting back to Chicago, I'm starting to see myself differently than when I was in LA."

"You were fine in LA. You don't have to change a thing. We were perfectly happy with the way things were going. Your kids will just complicate our relationship. Let their mother worry about them."

"Relationships are not that simple at times," Chris began to say when Candace interrupted him and said some friends had arrived, and she would be heading out for the evening.

The call ended, leaving Chris wondering about his relationship with Candace, his kids, and even with Elizabeth.

As Elizabeth was getting ready to go to sleep, she was thinking back about her praying with Linda. She couldn't remember when she prayed last, and she never prayed with someone else. She couldn't believe she did that. Also, she surprised herself by sharing her feelings about Chris with Linda. She wasn't sure what Chris thought about her now after a few years of being divorced. She also felt an unexplained urge to pray.

"Lord, I don't know what's happening to me. I always wanted to be in control and now realize I don't control my life, my kids, or my job. Please help me deal with so many problems. I know I haven't been to church in a long time, but I also know I can't do this by myself. I wonder if I should try to get my marriage back. Having Chris here has brought memories of the good times that our family had together. I guess what I'm saying is that I'm leaving it all in Your hands. Amen."

THIRTY-THREE

Hey guys, you're right on time. What do you want to do tonight?" Candace asked her friends after she hung up with Chris.

"We thought we would get something to eat and then go to this new bar," one of them said.

"Sounds great! Let me get my purse, and we'll be on our way," Candace replied.

The group drove to an upscale downtown restaurant. Even on a weekend, at night, it took almost an hour to get there. Upon arriving, the group got out, and a valet took the car to park. They entered a large lobby and a receptionist asked if they had reservations. After being assured that they did, the receptionist told them to be seated in the lobby while she checked on the table.

The room where they were seated was full of most guests dressed for a night out. Most of them were couples of various ages. Some looked like they were on a first date; others were probably celebrating wedding anniversaries of many years together. Candace and her friends were one of the few groups of women in the restaurant.

"So how are things going with Chris and you while he's

in Chicago?" one of her friends asked after they sat down for dinner.

"Things are going OK, I guess," Candace told them with hesitation.

"What do you mean by 'you guess'? I would be worried about him staying at his ex's house with his kids."

"I wasn't too worried about that. I mean, his wife is a lot older than me, and I'm sure I'm much more fun to be around and more attractive, although he talked about enjoying seeing some old friends. I think they were his neighbors."

"I'd be careful about that. Before you know it, he'll be dumping you and getting back together with his ex. Also, I'm not sure if I could go out with someone that old," another said.

"What do you mean by that?" Candace asked quickly.

"I mean you could be his daughter. I suppose there's some stability with an older guy that you don't get with some guy your age."

"That's funny. His doctor thought I was his daughter. Look, I really like Chris, or I should say I love him. We're thinking of moving in together when he gets back."

"Are you sure you're ready for that?"

"Sure, I'm sure. I mean we've been dating for a year now."

"Well, I wouldn't be too quick; he has had some health problems. That's what happens when these guys hit fifty. Everything is downhill after that!" her friend said with a laugh.

"Stop with that. Chris will be fine," Candace replied sharply.

"Have you thought that when you're fifty, he'll be seventy-five? Or when you are sixty-five, he'll be ninety?"

"I have thought about that, but I don't care," Candace said defiantly.

"Well, I'm just saying. A lot can happen over that much time," her friend said as their dinners arrived.

After dinner, the group split the check and headed out for the next stop on their night out. They arrived at a trendy bar in downtown LA about an hour later. One of Candace's friends, who was driving, stopped in front of the bar and everyone got out. A valet walked around to the driver's side of the car, and she handed him the keys along with a tip.

They entered a large room with a live band that played so loudly that they could barely hear each other talking. There was a large dance floor completely full of people in their twenties. There was also a very bright light show with light beams shining through the large room. They found a table near the back of the room so they could talk without yelling. A waitress stopped by for their drink order.

"Wow, there are a lot of single guys here. Maybe we should check out the crowd," one of her friends said.

"Go ahead, I'll just sit here, listening to the music and watching the crowd," Candace told them.

"You may want a backup plan if things don't work out with Chris," another one suggested sarcastically.

"I'm confident in my relationship with Chris. The rest of you go along, and I'll be fine here."

THIRTY-FOUR

A few nights later, Chris and Toby were sleeping on the couches in the family room. Chris had fallen asleep watching television. Toby got up and looked out the window and started to bark.

"Toby, be quiet." Chris yelled in a low voice, trying not to wake everyone up. He thought the dog saw some animal wandering around in the front yard. However, as he settled down to get back to sleep, he heard voices outside and then the door to the garage opened and closed. Chris got up and saw John coming in.

"Do you know what time it is?" Chris asked in a very low but stern voice.

"Yea, it's after one am, big deal," John replied nonchalantly, as he started to walk past Chris.

"Wait a minute. Don't you have to get up for school tomorrow?" Chris challenged him, as he grabbed John's arm.

"Hey, let go of me. This is none of your business. Besides, Mom doesn't care what time I come home. She doesn't stay up to check up on me."

"I am your father, and it is damn well my business!"

"Since when have you been acting like my father? Just because you are here for a few weeks doesn't change the fact that you abandoned us for a job in LA and some girlfriend half your age."

"What I do in my personal life is not your business. Your mother and I are divorced, and I can see whoever I want, just like she can. However, I am still your father. Who are those kids you were out with?"

"Just some friends I was hanging out with."

"Is that alcohol I smell on you?"

"We had a few beers out in the park. No big deal."

"First, you are underage for drinking. Second, you can develop bad habits and possible problems with alcohol."

"That's not going to happen. Everyone is doing it at school."

"I doubt everyone is."

"Well at least all the cool kids, not those nerds who study all the time."

"Based on what I heard from your mom, you could use some more time studying."

"I'll sure be glad when you are back in LA, then I can get in the house late and nobody notices."

"Well, I am going to talk with your mother about this and I expect you up and off to school on time tomorrow, even I if I have to get you there myself."

"Great, all I need is to be seen being driven to school by my father!"

"That should be motivation to get up on your own. Your mother and I will talk to you about this drinking and being out late tomorrow night when you are sober. Now get out of here and get some sleep!" Chris said angrily.

Chris went into the bedroom and tried to get some sleep.

He was thinking about his conversation with John. Maybe he hadn't been much of a father over the past several years. He wondered how much his absence contributed to John's drinking and partying late at night with his questionable friends. He decided to set his alarm on his phone to wake up before Elizabeth left for work to talk about John. He finally fell asleep with a late-night cable news program on.

The alarm went off at 6 am, and he realized it had been quite a while since he had been up that early in the morning. He heard Elizabeth downstairs in the kitchen and got his robe on quickly to catch her before she left. The kids were not yet down there.

"Hey, you're up early. I usually don't see you until I'm home after work," Elizabeth said, surprised to see Chris in the kitchen.

"I need to discuss something with you," Chris started to say.

"Can it wait until tonight? I'm running late for work already."

"It's about John. Do you know he stays out late and goes drinking with his friends?"

"Yes, I do, but I've talked with him about it, and nothing seems to work."

"You know about it!" Chris said almost shouting.

"Yes, but I can't control his actions. I've thought about getting him some counseling, but he refuses to consider it. I can't force him to go."

"So, you are OK with that?"

"No, I am not, but between working and keeping up on the housework, I just don't have the energy to do anything else."

"Why didn't you tell me about this?"

"Like what were you going to do about it from LA? You can't parent from long distance."

"I am still his father and have a right to know these things."

"How often do you call to see how things are going? "

"OK, you have a point. I am here now, so I will talk with him about it."

"I hate to admit it, but I could use the help. Now, I really need to get to work. Someone must pay the bills around here," she said with irritation as she headed out of the kitchen.

The kids came down for breakfast before heading to school. They asked about where their mother was, and Chris told them she had to leave early for a meeting. John barely made eye contact with Chris as he grabbed a banana and headed out of the kitchen and out the front door.

"What's with John?" Sarah asked.

"We had an argument last night," Chris told her and Jennifer.

"What was that about?"

"He came home at one in the morning and drunk, to put it bluntly."

"He does this regularly," Sarah said. "It's no big deal. I mean Mom never said anything, and I know she knows about it."

"What do you mean it's no big deal? Also, your mother told me she has talked with John about this, and he doesn't want to do anything about it."

"Lots of kids go out partying during the week. Some of my friends have asked me to go."

"So why don't you go if it's no big deal?"

"I don't want to get sick like I hear a lot of them do from drinking too much."

"I suppose that is one good reason," Chris said as he thought of how out of control his oldest two kids were becoming. "You and Jennifer better get going, or you'll both be late for school."

Sarah and Jennifer gathered their backpacks and headed out the front door to catch their school buses.

Chris started to think about what he would do today and realized he was getting into the same routine every day. He wondered how retired people deal with the monotony of not having a job to go to. *What do they do with all this free time?*

John talked with his friend Bob at school about his argument with Chris.

"My dad really got on my case last night when I came home. I wish he wouldn't fall asleep on the couch in the family room. He's got Jennifer's bedroom to sleep in," John told Bob.

"Hey, we really had a blast. Don't get down about your dad. He'll be back in LA soon with his hot girlfriend and won't be thinking about you back here in Chicago."

"Yea, my mom just ignores me when I get in late. I can do what I want. Besides, having a few beers isn't going to hurt anyone. I don't know why my dad gets so uptight about this. I'm sure he did some drinking when he was in school."

"Hey, remember there's a party this Friday with no parents around. It should be awesome! I heard the football cheerleaders will be there."

"That sounds great. I'll be there."

Later that day, Chris confronted John about his drinking when he came home from school.

"John, we need to talk," Chris told John as he entered the house. "Your mother and I are very concerned about your drinking and the friends you hang out with."

"Mom never said anything about it, so why are you worrying? It's not like you are here so much."

"I am still your father, and your mom is concerned. She told me that you refused to get any help."

"I don't need help. I can handle it."

"Maybe for now, but this could become an addiction," Chris said with genuine concern in his voice that surprised John.

"Look, Dad, I need to get some things done before dinner. Can we talk later?"

"Sure," Chris said resignedly as John left the room. He started to think about what Elizabeth said about not being able to parent long distance.

THIRTY-FIVE

At school the next day, Jennifer and Jessica met at lunch. "So, how'd you think the barbeque went?" Jessica asked as she and Jennifer sat down.

"Better than I expected. I think Emma Clark made an impression on my brother, John. He seemed to be really interested in getting to know her better. I think that's the only reason he's interested in going on the camping trip."

"Yea, I talked with Emma a couple of days ago. She thought John was OK, but she saw right through his interest in the camping trip. She did say that was all right with her. If it gets him coming to the youth group, she said she can handle his ulterior motives."

"I've noticed a lot of guys show up if their girlfriends are going to the meetings, but I don't really think she's interested in dating your brother. That reminds me, I don't know if my brother Michael noticed Sarah's interest in him. Sometimes he's not very observant."

"That may be true, but I know she must be interested in him if she wants to go to the camping meeting this Friday," Jessica observed. "Especially since I have noticed that she is very self-conscious of her image at school. I don't think going to youth group meetings are what the cool kids do."

"You mean we aren't the cool kids at school here?" Jessica asked sarcastically as both began to laugh.

"You know, why is going to church and being in a youth group not the cool things to do?" Jennifer asked, not expecting an answer.

"I don't know for sure. Some kids tell me that they think church is not fun and has too many rules. They can't see having a good time."

"What's having a good time? Partying and getting drunk? My brother does this and even Sarah gets on his case about it," Jennifer replied.

"Why does he do it? A lot of them just get sick after drinking too much."

"I don't know. It seems to have started when my parents were having problems. After they got divorced, it just got worse."

"What does your mom do about it?"

"Not much. She used to yell at him when he got home late at night after drinking, but she doesn't even wait up for him now. I think she doesn't know how to deal with it. She's busy with her job and keeping the house going."

"I don't know what my mom or dad would do if Michael came home drunk. I don't think it would happen again."

"Do they have rules for you and Michael?"

"None they talk about, but we just know where the boundaries are and don't cross over them."

"So why do you think most kids are not interested in church?" Jennifer asked again.

"OK, let me think about this a minute. Most of them think that having rules, like what Jesus teaches us, means we can't have fun. That's not true at all. One verse I always like is where He said He wants us to live life to the fullest. I don't think that means not enjoying life. But I think He is saying that we need to live as He lived. For me, that means not getting drunk with my friends. I don't like losing control of myself and I may do things I would not normally do."

"I agree. I know that some of them have gotten into trouble with the police for underage drinking."

"Worse, I have heard that some girls have sex with these guys while they're all drinking. That can lead to all kinds of things, like getting pregnant!" Jessica added.

"Yea, I don't know how they deal with that."

"For me, being cool is taking care of myself and not getting into stuff I will regret later."

"Me too. I sometimes think about what I want to do with my life and just hanging out and partying is not part of it," Jennifer agreed.

"Pastor Jim talks about how no one could live up to all the rules in the Old Testament, so Jesus came to earth and died for our sins. So, some of the kids think that you can do whatever you want since Jesus has it covered. But I don't think He wants us to just do whatever we want. I think the rules still apply because they also can protect us from ourselves, like getting sick from drinking too much or getting pregnant. I don't think anyone wants that to happen," Jessica said, getting back to the original question.

"Yea, I got to admit, I also thought that the kids in the youth group would be a bunch of nerds or just weird," Jennifer said in a hesitant voice.

"Thanks a lot!" Jessica said with a laugh, as she tried to sound insulted.

"No, I mean just the opposite. Because I knew you as a friend, I trusted you since you were not weird, I figured your friends at church would not be weird either. You know I was feeling bad about a lot of stuff and was willing to try anything, even Jesus. So, when you invited me to join your youth group meeting, I thought it couldn't hurt."

"Pastor Jim and the other pastors always remind us to invite friends to church. Most of the members in the church were invited by someone. You were the first person I invited to come to my group meeting. I was kind of nervous you would say no, and it would be awkward. I was so relieved when you said you would go."

"Of course, I said yes. I talked with you about how I felt and all the problems at my home. You listened to me, and I felt you really cared about me. I heard you talk about your faith and how Jesus related to everyone. How He helped people everyone else ignored. I kind of felt like some of those people were all alone, and no one was thinking about me. It sounded like Jesus might care about me. So, I decided to at least give Him a try."

"So, what did you think about the youth group after your first meeting?"

"Well, I thought everyone was friendly. I remember Pastor Jim's message that night. He was talking about how Jesus healed a crippled man who had been sitting at a pool for many years and everyone ignored him and would not help him into the water. Jesus went up to him and healed him.

Pastor Jim talked about how Jesus cares about all of us and listens to all our prayers. I started to think about how He might listen to me and help me. So, I decided to keep on going to the youth group meetings and services. I found other kids were like me with divorced parents or had other kinds of problems, I found I was not alone with my feelings."

"I knew the youth group and services were helping you. I could tell you were feeling better. I'm so glad I did invite you," Jessica told her.

"Me too. I don't know what would have happened to me without you getting me to meet Jesus."

"Hey, we better get to class before we're late," Jessica said being taken by surprise about how much impact inviting Jennifer to her youth group had on her life.

Sarah met Amy in the school cafeteria at lunchtime.

"It is very crowded in here today!" Amy told Sarah as they were walking with their lunch trays and looking for a table.

"There is a table with one person sitting there," Sarah pointed out to Amy.

"Are you crazy? We can't be seen near her, never mind sit with her for lunch," Amy said in a hushed and serious tone in her voice.

"What's wrong with her?" Sarah asked, somewhat surprised at Amy's response. The student sitting there was one of Sarah's friends from junior high school.

"That person is such a nerd. She studies a lot and always has the answers when a teacher asks the class a question," Amy told Sarah.

"Have you ever talked with her?" Sarah asked. She didn't want to tell Amy that she was a friend of hers in junior high school. Although she didn't want to hang out with her and other friends from junior high school, Amy's cruel comments still bothered her.

"No, why would I do that?"

"I don't know. Maybe she is not so bad, once you get to know her," Sarah suggested.

"Look, I see a table over there with a couple of friends we can sit with," Amy said, ignoring Sarah's comments,

"Hi guys. This is Sarah." Amy told the group as the girls sat down. "We were looking for a place to sit and only found a table with the weird girl that nobody talks to."

"Hi Sarah. So, are you a freshman?" one of the girls asked.

"Yes," Sarah said. She was not sure of how to fit in with Amy's friends.

"Hey Sarah, do you want to go out with us to the mall tonight?" Amy asked Sarah as they settled into eating lunch.

"Sure, that sounds great. It sure beats sitting at home and doing homework," Sarah told the group.

"That's for sure. I would rather be out with friends and have a good time," another one said.

"My parents are always bugging me about doing homework. I can't wait to graduate from high school and not have anyone hassling me about school," Amy told them.

"What do you want to do after high school?" Sarah asked her. She was thinking of her discussion earlier with her English teacher about her own career plans.

"I don't know. I guess I'll think about it after I get out of school," Amy told her with no concern.

In a few minutes Amy looked up at the clock. "We better get going, or we'll be late for classes," she told the group.

John met his best friend Bob and some other guys at lunch in the school lunchroom. This was the only time of the school day John enjoyed. They would sit and talk about their plans for the evening or weekend. This usually involved alcohol, parties, and girls.

John met Bob in his freshman year of high school. Prior

to that, he was best friends with Michael Chambers, who lived next door to him. Following the divorce, John and Michael had grown apart when John became more introverted,

John had no friends for a while until he entered high school. There he met Bob who provided John with diversions to his problems in terms of drinking and hanging out with students that had no interest in their own futures. John quickly became good friends with Bob and started to enjoy life again, if only for the wrong reasons.

"Hey, what's happening?" John asked as he sat down with his friends.

"Have you heard about the big party this weekend?" Bob asked him.

"No, but I'm always interested in the next party," John quickly replied.

"I heard it will be at a friend of a friend's home," Bob replied.

"Sounds good. Who all is going?"

"All the cool guys at the school."

"Any girls?"

"Of course. There will be kids from other schools also there. It will get crazy."

"Count me in on that one," John told them.

"Won't your mom hassle you about going out?" Bob asked him. "You tell me she has been getting on your case for being out late. It sounds like she isn't a fan of your friends, either."

"No problem. I'll just tell her I'm going to hang out at your house for the night. She never checks on my story. I think she likes to pretend it was true, so she doesn't have to argue with me," John said, surprised with himself about his insight into his mother.

"My parents never ask me about anything either. They're just too busy with their own stuff like work or going out with their friends," Bob said agreeing with John. "My dad is not home much with all his business travel and so I think my mother has enough to do with work and keeping up the house to check up on me. I guess she figured, as long I stay out of trouble, she's fine.

"You know my parents are divorced and my dad lives in LA. I don't hear from him very much. So maybe my mother is also too busy with things to worry about me," John said.

"Hi John," Michael Chambers said as he passed by the table where John and Bob are seated.

"Hey," John replied tersely.

"Isn't that Michael Chambers?" Bob asked John.

"Yea, that's him," he replied.

"What a nerd. He takes all these AP classes and is on the soccer team. He never wants to hang around with us. I invited him and his team to a party last year and only a few of them showed up. I think he thought he was better than me. In fact, a lot of the students like him look down on you and me, just because they do well in school," Bob told John. "How do you know him?"

"He lives next door to me," John replied hoping not to get into a long conversation about Michael Chambers.

"I didn't know that. Do you hang out with him?"

"Well, I used to when I was in grade school. But as you said, he's a nerd, and I just stopped hanging out with him. I think he's also into a church youth group. What a bunch of losers they must be," John told Bob.

"A church youth group! I bet they all look down on us, like we're not good enough to be their friends," Bob said with disdain in his voice.

"Hey, we better get going to the next class, or we'll get

hassled by the school principal's office for being late to class!" John said suddenly when he realized how much time had passed during lunch break.

THIRTY-SIX

Sarah got a call from Amy about plans for the weekend. "Hey Amy.

"Hi Sarah. I thought I'd call you about weekend plans."

"Great, I was also thinking about calling you about this weekend. "

"I was thinking about going to the mall on Friday night and hanging out there for a while. I heard there may be a party at one of the football players' homes. Maybe we can go check it out afterwards."

"Well, the mall sounds good, I don't know about the party," Sarah replied, forgetting about the youth group meeting she had committed to.

"What's wrong with the party?" Amy asked, incredulous that Sarah was questioning going to the party.

"I'm not sure about the party. Things can get out of control. I assume there will be beer there."

"Of course. Also, no adults either. The perfect match!" Also, some very cute guys," Amy said with anticipation.

"Don't you worry about things getting out of control? My brother John goes out with his friends and gets drunk. I think he and his friends have almost gotten arrested by the cops at one party for underage drinking. He told me they were able to get out just before the police showed up," Sarah said with apprehension.

"That's not going to happen here. The house is in that expensive area of town with lots of room between houses. No one will even know we're there. Besides, all the cool kids will be there. We're only freshmen, and we need to show we are as cool as them. Don't you want to be with the right group?"

"I guess. I don't know."

"What do you mean you don't know? The other choice is being one of the nerds who just study, don't party at all, and are just plain boring. I couldn't stand being one of them."

"Also, what will I tell my mom about getting home? She'll be dropping me off at the mall. Remember, we don't drive," Sarah said sarcastically.

"You do have a point there. I hadn't thought about that. OK, let's just go to the mall. Maybe see a movie," Amy said-with resignation.

"Sounds good to me," Sarah said with a sigh of relief. She couldn't believe how much discussion went into planning the night out! She was very happy not to go to the party. Sometimes she didn't know what she really wanted out of life and who she really was.

On Friday evening at dinner, the family sat around the dining room table eating dinner without much discussion. Jennifer reminded John and Sarah about the youth group meeting that evening.

"I forgot all about it. I already made plans with my friends," John said.

"Me too," added Sarah.

"You agreed to this last weekend. You should keep your

commitments and reschedule with your friends for another time."

"Well, I would like to see Emma again. I suppose my friends can wait," John said as he was thinking aloud.

"That reminds me that Michael will be there. Is that right, Jennifer?" Sarah asked hopefully.

"Yes, he'll be there. If that motivates you to attend, so be it!" Jennifer said, exasperated at her sister's shallow attitude.

"After further consideration, I'll call my friends to change plans," John declared.

"Me too. I really need to keep my commitments," Sarah said in a mocking tone.

John called his friend Bob about cancelling plans.

"Hey Bob, this is John. Something has come up, and I need to cancel our plans for tonight."

"Dude, you're going to miss a great party. Rich's parents are out of town, and everyone from school will be there."

"I know, but I met this girl I'll be seeing tonight," John said, only partly telling the whole story and misleading Bob.

"Wow, I guess you already have party plans for two. No need to explain further. I'll catch up with you on Monday at school. You can fill me in on all the details."

"Sure," John said, not sure what he would tell him on Monday. He'd worry about Monday on Monday.

Sarah called her friend Amy to cancel plans to go shopping at the mall.

"Hi Amy, this is Sarah. I forgot about another plan I had for tonight and need to cancel on going to the mall."

"So, what's happening?" Amy asked.

"Well, to tell you the truth, I am going to a church youth group meeting and possibly going on a camping trip. Since you are my best friend, I thought I would tell you but please don't tell anyone."

"No problem. So, what's with the youth group?"

"My little sister Jennifer goes to it, and this guy, Michael, who lives next door also goes to this group. He's hot and so I thought I might be able to get to know him better. Is that a lame reason to go?"

"I have heard some of my friends do stranger things to meet a guy than going to a youth group meeting."

"Well, that makes me feel a little better."

"Let me know how it goes on Monday at school."

THIRTY-SEVEN

When Linda drove the minivan into the Baldwin's driveway, the three Baldwin children came out and got in. It was a little cramped but acceptable for the short drive to Lakeside Community Church. They arrived at a separate building near the main church building that had a large auditorium for a sanctuary. As they entered the building, they saw a large room the size of a high school gym. A small stage was at the front of the room where a band was warming up. Near the entrance, Pastor Jim greeted them.

After saying hello to Pastor Jim, Michael and Jessica went into the auditorium and talked with some friends.

"Hi Jennifer. How has your week been going?" Pastor Jim Stone asked as he greeted her at the youth group meeting. "I see you brought a couple of friends."

"Oh, these are not my friends. I mean, we are friends too, but this is my brother John and sister Sarah."

"It is great to have you here tonight. As you may know, we'll be planning our youth group trip after the worship service. You're welcome to join us on the camping trip, if you're interested."

"That's why we came," John said hesitantly, not sure what

to say to a pastor. "Emma Clark and Michael Chambers told us about it last week. They said it was OK for us to go, even if we are not members of the church."

"No problem! A lot of the students here are not members, including their parents. Our church focuses on bringing people to God and serving in their communities, not so much on increasing membership rolls. However, we have many regular attendees who consider Lakeside Community Church their home church, even if they're not official members," Pastor Jim replied.

"That sounds great. By the way, have you seen Emma here yet?" John asked, more interested in Emma than what Pastor Jim had to say.

"Yes, she's over there with Michael and Jessica Chambers," Pastor Jim said, pointing to the far corner of the large auditorium. The building was used mainly for youth worship services and gatherings and was apart from the rest of the church building.

"You didn't say anything about there being a worship service at this meeting," John whispered to Jennifer as the three of them walked over to see Emma, Michael, and Jessica.

"You didn't ask. We have one every Friday night," Jennifer said, suppressing a laugh.

"I thought worship services were only on Sundays," Sarah added inquisitively.

"They have youth services on Friday nights and adult on Saturday and Sunday."

"I'm not sure about being at this worship service," John said.

"Look, you'll be fine. It's very casual, not like the ones at most churches."

"Well, I'm stuck here now, anyways. At least I may get a date with Emma by the end of the night. It wouldn't be a total loss."

"Really, is that all you came here for! I sometimes wonder who the oldest child in the family is," Jennifer said with disgust.

"Hi Emma," John said as soon as they met her and the others.

"Hey John. Nice to see you again. You too Sarah and Jennifer," she said, not to sound too interested in John, although she was curious about him.

"I'm glad you all decided to come," Michael told them. "Hey, better find some seats before the service starts."

The beginning of the services started with contemporary Christian rock-style music and light show. The students were on their feet singing and clapping, at times.

This feels more like a rock concert than a church service. I wonder if the worship leader who's leading the singers will fall back into the front seats like a mosh pit at a concert. John laughed to himself as he watched several teenage singers and musicians playing guitars and drums.

As he listened to the words that went with the music, he heard a completely different message than typical pop music provided. These were words of love and forgiveness. He wondered how many of the students listened to the words or just enjoyed the music.

After about fifteen minutes of music, announcements were made. Then Pastor Jim Stone got on the stage, the lights went up, and he began this week's teaching message.

"Tonight, I'm going to talk about God having a purpose and plan for each of your lives. I know as teenagers you're asked questions about what you're going to do after high school or what college you're going to. This last question already makes a statement about our culture valuing a college education. However, I believe there are other options to consider such as the trades including carpenters, plumbers, and electricians.

"So, how many of you have been asked these kinds of questions?"

A lot of students raised their hands.

"Now, how many of you know the answers to those questions?"

A lot again raised their hands.

This is not what I expected to hear, John thought as he also raised his hand to the first question surprising himself that he is that interested to take part in the response.

The pastor continued. "When I was your age, I started thinking about serving as a youth pastor, but I also considered majoring in business in college. So, as you can see, life can take us in very different directions. You may have been surprised to hear that God has a purpose and a plan for each of us. This is very clear from scriptures. Psalm 139:13 says: 'For you created my inmost being; you knit me together in my mother's womb." In this passage, David is saying God formed him and all of us, not only physically, but spiritually. God took a personal interest in him. He does so with all of us. So, it's logical to conclude that God also would have a plan for each of our lives. He cares about each of us.

"He knew all of us before we were known to our parents, before we were even conceived. I know as teenagers you may wonder what you will do after high school. Up to now, most things you have been told to do. There comes a time soon when you'll need to decide for yourselves what you will do. No one is going to tell you when to go to school, do homework, or do chores around the house.

"Most of you are fortunate to have parents that really care about you, and if you think they bug you too much, it is probably because they want only the best for you. Well, think of how much more God wants the best for each of you if He formed us and knew us from the very beginnings of our lives.

"So how do you honor God with your own behaviors? Who do you hang out with? Your future may well be tied to the friends you keep. I know some of your parents don't like your choice of friends. You know, your friends say a lot about you. Your friends can lead you down good and bad paths.

"You know it's very easy to be influenced by your peers. Let's say one of your friends gets their hands on a six pack of beer. A couple of them start to drink and put pressure on you to do so likewise. There's a lot of peer pressure to conform to the group. I get that. I remember times when I wanted to fit in with the cool crowd. They were the ones who seemed to have all the fun. You may have fun for the moment, but what is this doing for your future? Nothing. First Corinthians 15:33 says, 'Bad company corrupts good character.' This was true thousands of years ago and is still true now. The people you surround yourself with have the greatest influence on your lives. Your parents know this and therefore they may nag you about your choice of friends. God knows this too. He wants the best for you and that includes the people you call friends.

"In Psalm 139:16 (MSG) it says, 'The days of my life all prepared before I'd even lived one day.' So, again, God even knows every single day of our lives. This means that God does have a purpose and plan for each of your lives. I know some of you already know what you want to do and that's great. But I also know a lot of you don't really know what you want to do, and some of you aren't even thinking about the future yet.

"Parents sometimes come to me with concerns about their children not being at all interested in their futures. Some of you may be those children, or you have friends that don't seem interested in what they're going to do with their lives. Our lives are a gift from God, and each of us needs to decide what God's plan for our lives is and our purpose for existing. When we find out what God's plan is for us, I believe we're most successful."

This sure sounds like my dad! I wonder if he was thinking about God having a purpose and a plan for my life or just trying to give me a hard time, John wondered to himself as he listened to the message.

"Again, in Jeremiah 29:11 it says, 'For I know the plans I have for you,' declares the LORD, 'plans to prosper you and not to harm you, plans to give you hope and a future.' This is from a letter the prophet Jeremiah sent to the Jewish exiles. They were captured by King Nebuchadnezzar from Jerusalem and taken to Babylon. This was a message of hope and letting them know that the Lord had not forgotten them. He still had plans for them and a bright future. It was sent to encourage them to hang in there and better days were ahead.

"This is the same message for us today. If you feel like there is no future and you have done poorly in school, this message is for you. If you have gotten involved with drugs or alcohol, this message is for you. If you are hanging with bad company and have gotten in trouble with the law, this message is for you. If you are pregnant and don't know where to turn, this message is for you. If have serious family problems or divorce that is tearing you apart emotionally, this message is for you. The Lord has 'plans to give you hope and a future.'

"Don't give up. Your life matters to God, and He wants you to live it to the fullest. Jesus said in John 10:10, 'The thief comes only to steal and kill and destroy; I have come that they may have life, and have it to the full.' Being a Christian is about hope and living our lives to the fullest. You see, Jesus wants us to enjoy life and enjoy it to the fullest possible.

"God and Jesus are always there to help us. The thief is Satan, who is always trying to tempt us into failure and sin with our weaknesses. These can be our daily problems that we struggle with. We only need to reach out to Jesus in prayer and study what God is telling us in the Bible. I hope you can see from the few verses I cited tonight that the scriptures are just as pertinent to us today as they were thousands of years ago. We deal with the same struggles people have dealt with for centuries. We are not that different today as in the past.

"I have read the same verses many times, and they sometimes seem to mean something different each time I read them. Sometimes I have experienced a situation where the verse speaks differently than before I had that experience. I think you will also find this true as you continue to read familiar verses repeatedly during your lives.

"Proverbs 12:15 says, 'The way of fools seems right to them, but the wise listen to advice.' This is saying sometimes we all need to seek advice from those who care about us, even if we don't like what we hear. A foolish person does whatever he or she wants to do without regard to what anyone close to them has said.

"So, how do you apply this to figuring out what you want

to do after high school and what's God's plan for your life? Like the writer of Proverbs 12:15 said, seek advice. Talk to your parents, friends and maybe some teachers at school. Also, spend some time praying about it. God may give you some answers directly or through others you speak with. God uses all people to do His work.

"I want to talk to you about a young person that God chose to be the leader of the Jews. This person was David. When God sent Samuel to see Jesse to pick one of his sons for the next king, he first saw one of his sons that he thought was perfect to be the king from his outward appearance. But God said to Samuel, 'Do not consider his appearance or his height, for I have rejected him. The Lord does not look at the things people look at. People look at the outward appearance, but the Lord looks at the heart' (1 Samuel 16:7).

"You see, David was the youngest and not considered ready for such a large responsibility. However, he was the person God chose to be the next king over Israel. He was tending the sheep when Samuel asked to see him. This was a very lowly job in the family, certainly not for one worthy to be a king. Nonetheless, God chose David who became one of the greatest leaders of Israel.

"Does this sound familiar to any of you or someone you know? You cannot predict what you may become as an adult. David appeared to be the least likely person to be the leader of the Jews, but God used him for His own plans. This is exactly what God can do for any of you.

"So, no matter where you find yourself today, try to listen to what God, through the Holy Spirit and prayer, is telling you. Your dreams may not be exactly what God's plan is for you. So, pray about it and try different things. When you find the right thing, you'll know it by the energy and excitement you get from doing it.

"I hear some of you tell me that you can't do anything. You aren't good at sports and don't do well in school. Well, you have probably heard of the story of how David killed the giant Philistine Goliath. In fact, this story has become part of our culture when talking about one person suing a corporation it is like, 'David versus Goliath.' Well, in the biblical story given in 1 Samuel 17, David was thought too young and inexperienced in fighting to take on Goliath who was much older and an experienced warrior. However, David had confidence in himself, and that God was with him to help him. So, he went on to kill Goliath and rescue the Israelites from the Philistines.

"This is an example of the Israelites not trusting in God and becoming afraid when Goliath challenged them to send someone to fight him. In I Samuel 17:11 it says, 'On hearing the Philistine's words, Saul and all the Israelites were dismayed and terrified.' So, this happened to the Israelites, after knowing all God has done for them. So, it is easy for all of us to become dismayed at times and afraid to take on a challenge. This is when we need to pray to God and trust in him to support us.

"I could spend weeks talking about David who did many things good and bad, but in the end, he is considered one of the greatest leaders of Israel. In fact, in Acts 13:36 the Apostle Paul said, 'David had served God's purpose in his own generation.' So, God used David for His purposes just as God wants to use each of you for His purpose.

"Getting back to my own story, I thought I would like business, but I found that ministry is what really excites me and I find myself in the zone. I think it is good that you try different things and see what puts you in your own zone where you feel most comfortable and energized. I believe this is when you have found what God's purpose and plan is for your life.

"Let's pray as we end the service. Lord, please open our minds to your will for our lives and to allow us to learn Your plans and purpose for our lives. Help us to trust that You always have our best interests in mind and that You have known each of us personally since before we were born and will always be there for us. Amen.

"Let's take a break and get some snacks and drinks before meeting to discuss the camping trip," Pastor Jim announced as the service ended.

"So, what did you think about the service?" Emma asked John.

"It was not what I expected. I never thought about God knowing me personally. In fact, I'm not sure there is a God."

"Why is that?"

"Well, the pastor talks about God having a purpose and plan for each of us, but I don't see one for me. My parents have been divorced and Mom hasn't been the same since. My father hardly calls us from LA. I don't know if anyone really cares what I do."

"I felt that way after my father died."

"Wow! I'm sorry to hear that."

"It's been several years ago now, but I felt God had abandoned me. My mom also went through some tough stuff. He was killed in a car crash a few years ago.

"I remember my mom going over to your house to see your mother. It was just awful," Jessica added.

"Well, my family were not members of any church, and the Chambers knew us from school functions and said we could have the funeral at their church. We moved since but I started to get involved in the youth group here. Over time I realized that God didn't cause the accident, but He was there to help me get through it. I saw how Jesus had influenced other kids and their families in positive ways. I talked with Pastor Jim a lot about things, and I finally decided that I needed to trust Jesus and accepted him as my Lord and Savior. I was even baptized here."

"You got baptized! Was that weird?"

"No, in fact it was kind of cool. I walked into this small tank of water on the stage of the main auditorium, and the pastor asked me if I accepted Jesus Christ as my Lord and Savior. I said yes and he said, 'I baptize you in the name of the Father, Son and Holy Spirit.' Then I held my nose and leaned backwards as he dunked me under the water. When I got out of the water the people were applauding, and I could hear the worship band playing some music with singing. I felt like I had a new beginning after being baptized."

"So, what about your dad's death? Don't you blame God for it?"

"At first, I did. I wasn't sure why we were even having a funeral in a church. Over time I found that God did not cause the accident or any other bad things that happen. However, I did discover that God was there to get me through it."

"I'm not sure about all this stuff about God and Jesus. I did get to thinking about an argument I got into with my father a couple of days ago when I got home late as the Pastor talked about God having a plan for each of us."

"What was it about?" asked Emma.

"Well, in addition to getting in late, he found out I was drinking with friends and got really upset and mad. My dad said I needed to be careful who I hang out with and focus on school more. What's the big deal? He'll be gone again in a couple of weeks and won't care what I do."

"I don't know if that is true. I think he does care. Maybe he's seeing things differently since he has been back here."

"I don't know. Maybe. He does seem to be interested in getting to know us more and what we are doing. He and Mom also seemed to be getting along better than I expected. She was very upset after the divorce, and I think still is."

"One thing I have heard Pastor Jim say is that all things are possible with God," Emma suggested to John.

"Even if we don't believe He exists?"

"I think God works in a lot of different ways to reach people. Maybe that explains why you're here. You got invited by Michael and Jessica."

"I never thought about it that way. I am not sure about God caring about me."

"You don't have to be. Just come and see. This is all you can do and see what happens. I got to admit there was a time I was just like you when it came to God and Jesus. So, do you think you'll be back?"

"If you're here, I will be here."

"John, I can't believe you. After everything Emma just said, you're just trying to hit on her!" Sarah exclaimed with revulsion.

"It's OK. I figured that's why John came here in the first place. You really aren't that hard to figure out. Look, John, let's just keep things as friends. You have a lot going on in your life and the last thing you need is a girlfriend. However, I would love to have you and Sarah back regularly," Emma said with a smile.

"Well, I'll have to check my schedule," Sarah said. "But I

was interested in what kind of plans God may have for me. I really don't have a clue!"

"Also, maybe we could get to know each other better on the camping trip, if you're still interested?" Emma suggested to John in an attempt not to completely dump him in front of the others.

"Sure. To be honest, that's the reason I showed up here tonight," John replied sheepishly.

"Maybe God is using me to get to you! We better get over to the meeting to talk about it," Emma told them as she started to walk towards the auditorium exit, giving John an alluring look.

The group spent about an hour discussing the upcoming trip along with opportunities to serve the local community. Serving others was a large focus of the church, and Pastor Jim wanted the young people to develop a habit of serving regularly. The meeting was winding down, and everyone was heading for the front doors to leave.

"It's about time to leave. Let's head out. My mom is usually on time waiting for us," Michael told the group.

Linda was parked out front, and they all got into the van.

"How did it go for you all?" Linda asked as they started out of the large church parking lot.

"Better than I thought it would," John said candidly. "Emma told us about how her dad was killed in a car crash a few years ago."

"That was a difficult time for us. However, one good thing that came out of it, Emma's family got connected with our church. I think that helped them out."

"It sounds like what we heard tonight about God working through other people to reach them and having a plan for each of us," Sarah said with some astonishment in her voice at this thought.

"That's exactly right. I believe God is always there with a plan for us. The hard part is being able to listen to that plan. I know I get very busy with day-to-day things and don't spend enough time trying to listen to what God has to say to me," Linda told the group.

The group was quiet for most of the trip back home. Linda stopped in the Baldwin's driveway and John, Sarah, and Jennifer got out and headed for the front door.

"So, how was it?" Chris asked them as they entered the living room.

"OK, I guess," John said.

"Just OK?"

"Well, I did get to talk with Emma. She told me her dad died in a car crash a couple of years ago. They didn't go to any church, so the Chambers offered their church for his funeral. That's how she started going there. She became a Christian and even was baptized!"

"The pastor talked about how God has a plan for each of us," Sarah added. "I don't know what I want to do and how am I supposed to figure out what God wants for me?"

"I got to admit, I'm not sure God even exists," John told them.

"I tend to agree with you. My life hasn't gone as I had planned," Chris replied.

"Look at our marriage. I don't think our divorce was part of any plan I had," Elizabeth added to the conversation.

"Don't you guys get it?" Jennifer started. "You are all focused on yourselves and what you want and not what God wants. That's what I finally figured out after going to Lakeside Church for a while."

"If God knows what's best for all of us, why do we have all these problems?" John asked.

"It's because we're not doing God's will for us. We're doing what we want," Jennifer replied.

"So how do I figure out what God wants?"

"I pray about things and read the Bible. That's what Pastor Jim was talking about."

"Why would God listen to me? That is if He exists at all. How do you know He is even there?"

"This is not something you can prove like a math problem or scientific experiment. It comes down to faith, but I always think there are things hard to explain without God."

"Like what?"

"Well, like how did the universe come to be. It couldn't start with nothing. With God, this is easy to explain; without God, it seems impossible to explain creating something out of nothing."

"That's something like the Big Bang Theory we studied in my astronomy class."

"You see, science and faith can be compatible," Jennifer concluded with a smile.

"I'll have to think about this for a while," Sarah told them.

"So, what do you make of our kids' conversation about God?" Elizabeth asked Chris after their children had gone to their bedrooms.

"I don't know. I really haven't thought about God in quite a while. I have been too wrapped up with life day to day to think about anything else."

"Me too. I'm glad to see Jennifer finding something to believe in. It seems to be giving her more focus than the other two kids who seem to have no focus for their lives. I am especially concerned about John. He'll be a senior next year and has no idea what he wants to do after high school, and his grades are terrible."

"I agree and will try to reach out to him. It's been hard with only being around here for a few weeks," Chris said without a clue about how he would talk to John. "So, what about us? Do you think that God did not care about our marriage?"

"I don't know what to think about God. Jennifer sounds so sure about all of this. We never thought much about attending a church when we were married. So why even think about it now? It's too late, right? We're divorced, and nothing can be done about that."

"Yea, even God can't change that, right? The court was clear about it. We signed all the documents splitting assets and deciding child custody."

"It seems like we had so many problems that even God could not work it out."

"Could not or would not," Elizabeth asked.

"What do you mean by that?"

"I don't know. Maybe if we prayed about it. We did have some good times along with the bad."

"You're right about that. Sometimes I forget why we really got divorced."

"Me too. Well, we can discuss this more in the morning. Good night."

"Good night. I think I'll just read a little bit here before turning in," Chris said with a similar thought.

"Hey Dad, can we talk?" John asked after his mom had left the room.

"Sure. What's on your mind?"

"Well, I got to thinking about the other night when I came home late. I guess you may be right about my drinking and my friends. I just have trouble thinking about the future. It's easier just having a good time with my friends instead of spending a lot of time studying."

"Well, I only got upset because I care about you. No matter what happens between your mother and me, you will always be my son."

"Tonight, the pastor talked about God having a purpose and a plan for each of us. I don't know if I believe that, but I do believe you."

"I'm not sure about what God thought either, but I'm glad you believe I care about you. For that matter, I care about Sarah and Jennifer too. I have come to realize that I haven't been a very good father to you, and I need to make some changes."

"Well, I guess I need to make some changes too. See you in the morning," John said as he left the room surprised at his father's admission.

THIRTY-EIGHT

Chris got back to reading the paper. He started to fall asleep in the wing back chair when his cell phone buzzed.

"Hi. How's it going there?" Candace said to Chris.

"Well, the kids all went to our neighbor's church tonight. They came back talking about what God's plan is for their lives. I guess that was the topic of the pastor's sermon."

"Who believes in God? Like you can't see Him or hear Him. Look at all the bad stuff that happens out there. If there is a God, why does He let all the bad stuff happen?"

"I agree; I don't think much about a higher being out there. So, how are things in LA?

"I miss you. I'm still traveling some, but it's getting lonely here."

"A couple more weeks and I'll be back there. I think my incisions are healing well, but I am having real problems with eating much food. If I eat more than a small amount, I get really bad pain in my abdomen. My doctor has me on a soup and stew diet for a few days. He said to try other foods after that and see what happens. A couple of nights ago, I was in enough pain that I took a Vicodin. I didn't use them much right after the surgery for pain from my incisions."

"Well, I hope you're well soon. This seems to be dragging on."

"I got to admit, I thought I would be doing better at this point. My doctor said everyone is different. At least I have lost some weight, almost twenty pounds."

"We should go shopping for some new clothes when you get back here."

"I guess so, if I keep the weight off."

"Hey, I must go. I'm meeting some friends at a new club. They seem to like having me single for a while. They see more of me."

"Have a good time, but not too good a time. If you know what I mean?"

"I think so. Love you."

"Love you too," Chris said as he finished the call and was not sure if his last comment was true anymore.

THIRTY-NINE

On Monday, John was having lunch at school with his friend Bob in the cafeteria. It was arranged like a food court in a shopping mall with several themed food areas. John and Bob returned from separate areas with their trays and found a table to sit down.

"You really missed a great party this past weekend. Everyone from school was there and there were no parents around to tell us what to do or what to drink. A couple of the seniors got some beer with their fake IDs. The girls there were awesome! Everyone had a great time. You should've been there."

"That reminds me, how was your date?" Bob asked, wanting to know what he expects to be all the sordid details.

"It went OK," John replied factually, having forgotten he told Bob he had a date with Emma and was not just meeting her at the youth group meeting. He would never have heard the end of it if he told him the truth.

"What do you mean by 'OK'? Was she hot? Do I know her?"

"No, you don't know her; she goes to another high school."

"How did you meet her?"

"She's a friend of a neighbor of mine, Michael Chambers."

"Michael Chambers the nerd. That guy is so boring. All he does is study and play soccer. I think he's even in a church youth group," Bob said very quietly.

"Yea, I think he's in a youth group. What does that matter?"

"He never parties with the rest of us. I think he figures he's better than us."

"Just because he doesn't want to go out and get drunk every weekend doesn't mean he's judging you," John replied, realizing he was now defending Michael.

"Hey, don't get so uptight. You like to put a few beers down on the weekends. Are you hanging out with him?"

"Not really. But remember last week I told you I got into a big argument with my dad about coming home late and drunk. I forget he's around at times. Since the divorce, he left for a job in LA, and he has a girlfriend. He's back for a few weeks, recovering from surgery. My mom is too tired to stay up and wait for me to get home, so I guess I've gotten used to doing what I want."

"He has a girlfriend? Is she hot? I heard there are a lot of hot girls in LA."

"I have never met her or seen a picture of her, but from what my mom said I think she's about 25 years old and pretty hot looking."

"Wow, it sounds like your dad has moved on."

"That's what I thought. Now that he's been home for a while, I'm not so sure."

"At least it must be great not having to have any parents bothering you. My mom and dad are always on my back about my partying."

"Maybe they just care about you," John replied with his new perspective of his parents.

"I doubt it. I think they just want to give me a hard time."

Looking at the wall clock, John got up quickly and said, "We better get going before we're late for class." John was glad for the diversion so he could end the conversation.

Amy saw Sarah in the cafeteria and at once sat down to see what happened to Michael and Sarah over the weekend.

"So, how did it go with Michael?" Amy asked.

"It went OK, I guess. It was kind of hard to talk with him a lot with several other people there," Sarah replied.

"I think I know him from the boys' soccer team. A guy I used to date is on the team. Are you going to see him again? Did he ask you out for a date?"

"Probably, but he did not exactly ask me out for a date. I'm not sure he even knew I was interested in him. He probably thought I went to the meeting because I was interested in the group. So, that approach didn't work very well." Sarah sighed.

"He is kind of cute," Amy replied. "He doesn't like to party with some of the guys on the team if I remember right. So, I might find him boring. However, if you like him, sometimes you just must be direct with a guy. They don't read signals very well. The guys I usually hang out with seem to read the wrong signals!" Amy joked. "Michael seems different that way." Suddenly changing the subject, Amy asked, "Was it weird being at the youth group meeting? I've never been to one, but it sounds like a boring way to spend time."

"That's what I thought going in. But I heard some interesting stories from the other kids about why they're there. It seems like a lot of them have problems like I do. Some are even worse. There is this one girl, Emma, whose father died in a car crash a few years ago. At least I still have a father, even though he doesn't live with us anymore."

"My parents fight all the time. I think it would be better if they got divorced."

"I used to think that before my parents got divorced. They argued a lot too. But things seemed to change a lot afterwards. I think I'd rather have them together, even with all the fighting." Sarah replied with a sense of appreciation of how life used to be for her family.

The bell rang, signaling it was time to get to the next class. Sarah and Amy dropped off the trash from their trays, placed them on the moving conveyor belt, and headed to their classes.

Jennifer and Jessica met after school at Jennifer's house.

"What did John and Sarah think about the youth service?" Jessica asked as she and Jennifer sat on the couch in the basement rec room watching a movie.

"I think John was more interested in Emma. I couldn't believe how he hit on her after she told the story about her dad being killed in a car accident. I'm not sure if he got anything out of the service. I think he only went there to try to get a date with Emma."

"That may be true, but he still showed up. Pastor Jim can be very persuasive with his teachings. I bet he found something interesting to think about. I noticed he was really listening."

"My sister Sarah also came because she likes your brother. I don't think he really noticed her interest in him."

"Michael can be kind of clueless when it comes to girls. Maybe he'll have a good influence on her. You told me your mom doesn't like her friends very much."

"Yea, she thought they're too interested in dating and not

enough interest in school and going to college. She would approve of what Pastor Jim was telling us about God having a purpose and plan for each of us."

"What do you think about God having a plan for each of us?" Jessica asked.

"I'm not sure. I really don't have any idea what I want to do with my life. My siblings don't know either. Pastor Jim talked about God knowing each of us before we were even born. I have trouble understanding this. What does this mean?"

"I think that God knows us each personally. I guess that's why Pastor Jim talks about God having a plan for each of us. I don't know either what I want to do with my life, but I don't want to waste it. That's one thing that I found cool about God. He personally knows me."

"I agree, having that kind of relationship makes me not feel alone. After my parents divorced, I felt like I was the only person to feel abandoned. Jesus cares about everyone. That helped me get through a lot of stuff. I wish my siblings could understand that."

"Have you tried to talk with them?"

"Yea, but they just blow me off. I think they want to handle everything themselves. I found when I asked Jesus for help, I didn't have to worry about how things will work out. I think they're hiding from their problems by drinking and partying."

"I think a lot of kids do that. Some tell me that being a Christian has too many rules and that it's boring to be one."

"I used to think that when you first invited me to Lakeside church. But I found I have more freedom. I try to trust Jesus with my problems and not worry so much. I do still get down at times, but I try not to do it too much."

"I also let things get to me at times. I'll keep your family in my prayers."

"Thanks, I know we really need all the prayers we can get!"

FORTY

Elizabeth decided to leave work early and stop by to talk with Linda. It had been a couple of weeks since they last talked, and she missed the conversations she used to have with her. After getting home, she called Linda to see if she was available.

"Hi Linda, this is Elizabeth. If you have time, are you available that I could stop by for coffee?"

"Sure."

"I got home early and still have some time before thinking about dinner. Maybe Chris will start dinner if I'm not doing it? No, that's not going to happen, but I can use the break."

"Great, I'll see you here soon."

After Elizabeth arrived, they went out to the screened parch in the backyard to have coffee and talk. The porch looked out on a manicured lawn with trees and a garden.

"So, how are things going with you and Chris?" Linda directly asked without any small talk.

"OK. In fact, I think we're starting to get along again. Certainly better than where we were at the time of our divorce. I'm not sure you know that he has been dating someone in LA for a while."

"No, I didn't know that," she said with surprise.

"She's half his age and great looking, from what I can gather. I think this is called an 'upgrade.' I'm not sure how serious it is. Chris is probably just having a good time being single. I'm still dealing with the failure of our marriage. I can't imagine dating right now. Also, I have kids to deal with. When would I have time for dating anyway? I told Chris about our prayer session last week."

"What did he say?"

"He didn't think it would help much. I must admit I'm not sure either. However, I have been praying for my family since we prayed."

"Does Chris know that?"

"No, I haven't told him about it. I think he'd say it is a waste of time."

"It isn't a waste of time. One thing to know is that God works on His time not ours. So be patient and keep on praying. There are lots of examples of people in the Old Testament waiting a long time for God to answer their prayers. The thing they all had in common was they stayed faithful to God's promise He would be there for them."

"Thanks, I will."

"Say, why don't you and Chris join Paul and me for worship services this Saturday night? The kids can come too. We can get together for dinner afterwards. There's a great pizza place nearby with locally brewed beers."

"I'm not sure about Chris being interested in attending a church service, but he won't be able pass up pizza and beer. I think he's eating better lately. It's taken quite a while for him to get his appetite back. He has lost about 20 pounds. I hate to say it, but the surgery made him look a bit more attractive."

"Have you told him that?"

"Are you kidding? I'm not sure where our relationship is these days, so I am very careful about what I say."

"Maybe you're too careful. What are you afraid of?"

"I don't know. Even though our divorce was hard on me, I have now gotten used to the way things are. I'm not sure I have the energy to try to regain it."

"Well, think about trying to. This may be the Holy Spirit nudging you," Linda suggested with a smile.

"I'm not sure about that, maybe it's just the weight loss!" Elizabeth said with a soft laugh. "Anyway, I should be starting dinner. We'll take you up on your invitation and see you this Saturday for church and pizza," Elizabeth said as she got up to leave.

"Great, we'll see you then," Linda replied.

While Elizabeth was at Linda's house, Chris decided to call Sam and see how things were going.

"Hi Sam, this is Chris."

"Hey Chris, how are you doing?"

"I'm doing OK. The only issue left for me is getting back to eating normally. I still get constipated if I eat too much food, but it's slowly getting better. My doctor said this part of the recovery varies with each person. I think I should be good to go by the end of next week. I can't believe I've been out of work for over four weeks."

"Well, you better not stay out too much longer. I hear things have been going well with Joe. He completed the deal with the Europeans, and your clients get along well with him. In fact, I was in a meeting with Don who commented that Joe has made your absence not noticeable. I would be concerned about that promotion. I'm sure Joe is on the short list with you."

"I can't believe this. I had that job in the bag before this surgery. I don't understand how this can happen. Everything seems to be out of my control!" Chris said irritated.

"How are things going with your kids and ex?"

"At first things were rough. I can't really blame them. I haven't been involved in their lives much. However, lately I think I'm getting along better with the kids and even with Elizabeth."

"Really, that is truly a miracle. I thought you and she would barely speak to each other."

"That's funny you said that. The youth pastor at the church Jennifer goes to said that God has changed people's lives in forty days. He said my being out of work for six weeks is about forty days. Maybe he's onto something. You never know where life will lead us."

"Hey, I got to get to a meeting so I'll talk with you later. Take care."

"Let's get out for a round of golf when I'm back."

"That sounds good to me," Sam said as he ended the call.

"How are things at work?" Elizabeth asked Chris as she walked into the family room. She had overheard Chris talking with Sam.

"Unbelievable! Sam told me that Joe has made my absence unnoticeable according to our boss, Don. I was hoping for just the opposite so my value to the company would be extremely obvious."

"As the saying goes, 'everyone is expendable,'" Elizabeth responded, trying to lighten up the conversation.

"Well, I guess this is really true for me."

"Look, you can't control what happens while you're away. I must admit your stay here has improved things a bit. Even we are starting to get along like the old days," she said encouragingly.

"We have been talking instead of yelling at each other," Chris agreed with a smile.

"I think the kids are also noticing we are getting along better, and they feel better about themselves," Elizabeth noted.

"Hey, can I ask you for some advice?" John said as he entered the family room during their conversation.

"Sure, what's on your mind?" Chris said.

"I know I'm in my senior year and things have not gone very well, to say the least. I'm starting to think I should be making some plans for after high school, but I really don't have a clue. It's kind of funny, but at the youth group meeting, the pastor was talking about teenagers needing to have plans for their future. He said that God has plans for all of us. I'm not sure about that, but he did suggest we talk with our parents for advice. Well, I got to thinking about all of this and decided I need to think about my future."

"That's great. It's never too late. So, what interests you?" Chris asked.

"I'm not sure. I do need to get my grades up before any college will look at me. I'm thinking of going to a community college for a two-year degree, get better grades, and figure out what I really like to do before applying to four-year colleges."

"It sounds like you already have it figured out. I think that is a great plan!" Elizabeth said to him.

"I agree with your mother," Chris said with a smile.

"I know you have been bugging me about making plans

and I've just ignored you. I think I've been a little scared about not having any plans and didn't want to face it. Pastor Jim said a lot of us don't know what to do after high school and acting like I didn't care made me feel better, like I'm not alone."

"It sounds like you got a lot more out of the youth group meeting than you went there for," Chris observed.

"The only thing I didn't get was a date with Emma, which was the real reason I went. She told me I have too much going on to have a girlfriend right now."

"I think Emma is wise beyond her years," Elizabeth said, reinforcing Emma's comments.

"Yea, I guess she's right too," John admitted hesitantly.

"I wonder if we should have been active in church years ago. I can't believe how much John got out of the meeting," Chris told Elizabeth after John headed out to see some friends.

"That's funny you said that. Linda invited us to join her and Paul for their Saturday worship service this week. I told her we would love to go. As far as John goes, I think he's been thinking about his future for a while and the pastor's comments were well timed to push him over the edge on his decisions. Maybe it's not coincidental that he went to that youth group meeting."

"Now you're starting to sound like Pastor Jim. After how well the kids are doing, I guess we could give it a try," Chris said as he wondered what was going on with his family. "Will the kids agree to go?"

"We'll discuss it at dinner tonight."

FORTY-ONE

After everyone was settled at the dinner table Elizabeth announced they would be going to worship services next Saturday with the Chambers family.

"Linda Chambers invited us to go with them to this Saturday's worship services at their church. I told we'd love to go."

"I don't know about that," John said in protest. "The youth group meeting was OK, but a church service can be extremely hard to keep awake during.

"Will Michael be there?" Sarah asked.

"I think the whole family will be there," Elizabeth replied, thinking whatever it took for the kids to go would work for her, knowing Sarah liked Michael.

"John, maybe you'll see Emma there," Sarah teased him.

"After the service, we'll go out for pizza at the place that uses brick ovens," Elizabeth added, trying to entice John.

"If you put it that way, I guess I can handle the service," he said, agreeing to go to the relief of Elizabeth who wasn't in the mood for a long argument on the pros and cons of attending a church worship service.

"That's great," Jennifer said. "We'll all be together for once. I enjoy going with the Chambers family, but it will be nice to go with my own family." She was really excited about doing something for a change as a normal family.

FORTY-TWO

Later that week, Bob called John about going to a party on Saturday night.

"Hey Bob, what's happening?" John asked his friend after he picked up the call and saw his name on the caller ID.

"I just wanted to tell you about another great party this Saturday night. I know you missed the last one for a date, but I figured you wouldn't want to miss another. There will be plenty of girls to go around, so don't worry about bringing a date."

"I don't think I can make it, since I have other plans," John said, although he wasn't sure how to tell him about going to a church service.

"I bet you have another date with that friend of nerd Michael Chambers. If she hangs out with him, she's probably not into partying either. She's probably just boring. You need to meet some girls that love to party and are fun to be around."

"Well, I don't think she does party much. But you know she seemed cool to hang out with. You know not everyone needs to be a partier to be cool."

"I don't know about that. So, what does she do for fun?"

"I don't know that much about her. She goes to a youth

group at Lakeside Community Church where Michael Chambers' family attend."

"Now I know she must be completely boring! Those Jesus freaks can be nerds and look down on everyone else."

"Look, she's not a Jesus freak, and she doesn't look down on everyone. Her dad died in a car accident, and Michael's family had the funeral at their church. That's when Emma and her family started to attend. She told me her faith in Jesus helped her get through a lot of tough stuff she was dealing with."

"Man, she already has you getting into this Jesus thing after hearing her story about her dad dying in an accident and how Jesus helped her feel better. I think these Christians take advantage of people like her when they are down to get them into their churches."

"The reason I can't go to the party is I'm going with my family and Michael's family to a service at their church Saturday night," John told Bob, not caring about what he thought after his callous comments about Emma.

"Like I said, I think these Christians take advantage of people like her when they're down to get them into their churches."

"That's not true. After getting to know her a little, I'm starting to think about Christians a little differently. I must admit, I thought the same way you do before meeting her. Her story is real, and getting into church really affected her. She's not just trying to sell me on Jesus. It's real to her, so I'm simply curious about what this is all about."

"You better be careful, or you'll become just as big a nerd as Michael. I won't tell the other guys about you going to church this Saturday instead of going to the party. They probably wouldn't talk with you again."

"You know what, Bob, I really don't care if you tell them or what they think. Maybe you and they are the ones looking down on anyone who is not like you. Think about it," John said as he hung up on Bob. He couldn't believe how insensitive his friend was about Emma. He also couldn't believe how he defended her, even though he hardly knew her.

"Hi Amy," Sarah said as she answered her call.

"I was calling about plans for Saturday night. We haven't gone out for a couple of weeks, so I thought you may be interested in going to the mall and checking out the guys. Maybe get something to eat too."

"You won't believe this, but I'm going to a worship service at Michael Chambers' church."

"You must really like him to go to a service. Those can be so boring. I think you would have a lot more fun checking out the guys at the mall."

"You may be right. I don't think Michael even noticed my interest in him at the youth group meeting. I don't know why I'm even interested in him. There are plenty of cute guys out there, even at the mall," Sarah said as she wondered why she agreed to go to the service.

"I would never go to a church service, no matter how great the guy is. Church is for old people. I don't see how it has anything for me."

"Like I told you about the youth service, I could relate to the stuff the pastor talked about. I didn't expect that. I figured it would be some boring stuff that I couldn't get my head around. The stuff in the Bible happened thousands of years ago. so I also thought, 'How could I relate to any of that?' Even though I'm probably going because Michael will be there, I'm a little curious about what they talk about at the service."

"If you ask me, I would choose going out with my friends over going to a service. Are you sure this Michael is worth the trouble? There are lots of other guys to choose from."

"I don't know. I can't figure out why I'm so interested in him. He's not like most of the guys we hang out with."

"Just be careful or before you know it you'll be getting married right after high school and having lots of kids!" Amy joked with her.

"No way! I don't plan to get married until I'm old, like thirty or more. I want to go to college and get a job making lots of money. After what happened to my parents, I'm not sure I want to get married. I think part of their problems was my mom and dad both having big career plans. I have big plans, and I certainly won't let any guy stop me from doing what I please."

"I guess I can agree with you on that one. If you do get serious with Michael, make sure he knows your plans too. Let me know how your exciting date at church goes on Monday."

"I will and don't do anything I wouldn't do this weekend," Sarah told Amy as she ended the call.

"I can't believe our two families are going to your church this Saturday," Jennifer told Jessica at lunch at school on Friday.

"I was surprised to hear your siblings agreed to go. I assumed they usually hang out with their friends on Saturday nights."

"That's true. I know Sarah likes your brother Michael even though he didn't seem very interested in her. So, I figure she thought this would be another chance to get his attention."

"Don't tell Sarah this, but Michael did tell me he was

happy Sarah was coming to the service. He didn't say why, but he usually doesn't say much at all, so I think he likes her," Jessica said in a low voice, pretending no one overheard them.

"Really, I'll try to keep that a secret. If I told Sarah, I don't know how she would react. Also, I do know John likes Emma. He probably hopes to see her there. I'm not sure these are good motives to go to church."

"Maybe God is using Michael and Emma to get your siblings to come and hear what He has to say to them at the worship services. There are Old Testament stories about how God used people for His own purposes."

"I don't know. Using dating to get people into church seems a little extreme to me."

"I agree, but I won't pretend to know what God is thinking," Jessica said, not sure what was really going on. "How are things going with your parents?"

"They seem to be getting along better since my dad came to Chicago. They seem to enjoy talking with each other, and my dad is relating to us better. I was glad when he came to stay with us, although my siblings really weren't very happy about it. But now, they seem to be talking with him more, and things seem more like they were before my parents got divorced."

"I'm glad to hear that. Do you think he might decide to stay instead of going back to Los Angelos?"

"I wish he would stay. I even pray to God that he stays, and they get married again. I think that would take a miracle, and even I am not sure God could pull that one off."

"Don't say that. You know that Pastor Jim said that all things are possible with God."

"You're right. Even if my parents don't get remarried, I need to trust that God is with me, and I will get through anything that happens."

FORTY-THREE

One late Saturday afternoon, the Baldwin family was getting ready to go meet the Chambers at Lakeside Community Church. As usual there was a lot of confusion before they all went out together.

"How long are you going to be in the bathroom?" Jennifer yelled through the door to Sarah.

"Just a couple of more minutes."

"You do know we are all going with you to see Michael and his family, and this is not a date with Michael?" Jennifer teased.

A couple of minutes later Sarah opened the door and said shortly, "I'm done." She then quickly headed downstairs.

"So, what should I wear for the service?" Chris asked Elizabeth as he stuck his head into her bedroom.

"I'm not sure. Let me ask Jennifer."

Elizabeth left her bedroom and went down the hallway to Jennifer's bedroom at the end of the hall.

"Jennifer, I have a question for you," she said as she knocked on the door.

"Come on in," Jennifer said.

"What should your father and I wear for the church service? We haven't been to church in a long time."

"Blue jeans are fine."

"Are you kidding? People wear blue jeans to church?"

"Sure, the pastors all wear jeans, even the senior pastor who will be giving the teaching. By the way, the teaching part usually goes about forty-five minutes."

"I guess it has been a while since I've been to church. That seems like a long time speaking by the pastor."

"He usually has an interesting message that I can relate to, so I don't notice the time."

"What does teaching mean? Is that what we used to call a sermon?"

"I think so. Anyway, I think you and dad will have a good time there."

"I never thought of having a good time at church. When I was a kid and went to church, it was something I had to endure and couldn't wait for the service to end."

"I think you'll find this different than the old days."

"We'll see. Also, I'm not that old!" she said with a grin.

Elizabeth headed back to her bedroom and told Chris what to wear.

"According to Jennifer, they're very casual at this church. Most people wear jeans, including all the pastors."

"Well, that will be a change in the right direction. I remember having to wear a suit to church when I was a kid."

"I also remember getting dressed up for services. However, I think I may wear a causal skirt since we are going out for the first time in a long time as a family."

"You always look great in a skirt or dress, so that works for me," Chris said with a smile.

"Are you flirting with me?"

"I don't know, maybe just a little bit. We may be divorced, but I can still appreciate you."

"I guess we're making progress!" Elizabeth exclaimed, completely shocked by Chris' compliment to her.

The family arrived at the church about ten minutes prior to the service. There were people in the parking lot directing traffic because a typical service would have over 2000 in attendance. The building had no resemblance to a traditional church. They were greeted at the doors and entered a large atrium with a bookstore and coffee shop nearby. Linda Chambers was waiting for them in the atrium and came over to greet them.

"It's great to see you again," Linda told the Baldwin family as she met them in the church atrium. "The service will start soon and with two families here we'll need to scout out several seats that are together."

"That sounds good. Thanks again for inviting us. The kids enjoyed the youth group meeting last week, and this will give Chris and me a chance to see your church also," Elizabeth told them.

Shortly after getting seated the lights went down and the worship team started the service with contemporary Christian music and a light show that seemed more like a rock concert to Chris and Elizabeth. They were used to a very traditional, low-key service.

"I'm waiting for the lead singer to fall back into the crowd like the mosh pit at a rock concert," Chris said to Elizabeth, as he was almost shouting over the music which was very loud.

"That's what I thought at the youth service," yelled John after overhearing his father's comments.

"I guess we still have a few things in common," Chris replied with a smile.

After the music and announcements were done, the senior pastor, Pastor John Walker, began his message for the service.

"Tonight, I'm going to talk about relationships and what the Bible tells us about them.

I wonder where this is going? Considering my own situation right now, maybe I'll find some words of wisdom, Chris thought as the pastor began his message:

"You know there are hundreds of laws in the Old Testament about human behavior. Many will tend to use some of these to point out flaws in others, and who is justified and who is sinful. I am reminded of the expert in Jewish law asking Jesus which is the greatest commandment in the Law in Matthew 22. Jesus replied in Matthew 22:37-40, 'Love the Lord your God with all your heart and with all your soul and with all your mind.' This is the first and greatest commandment. And the second is like it: 'Love your neighbor as yourself.' All the Law and the Prophets hang on these two commandments.'

"These commandments are from two Old Testament laws: Deuteronomy 6:5 and Leviticus 19:18. The expert in Jewish law was trying to test Jesus. I'm sure he, like many others, was aware of these two laws. Perhaps it took Jesus to point them out to him and us because it's harder to love God and our neighbor than to point out our neighbor's faults. But isn't that what Jesus continues to challenge us to do, behave counter to the culture?

"Notice the key words in each begin with love, 'Love the Lord your God' and 'Love your neighbor.' So, before we begin to rack and stack all the folks out there, we need to keep in mind that loving God and loving people trumps all other law. This is clearly said in Luke 6:37 Jesus said 'Do not judge, and you will not be judged. Do not condemn, and you will not be condemned. Forgive, and you will be forgiven.'

"You know the outside world is quick to point out Christians as being very judgmental. I think Jesus was aware of how human nature is quick to put down others for various reasons without considering our own faults. None of us live up to the standards set by Jesus.

"Jesus also makes it clear that none of us lives up to any of the Law. For instance, in Matthew 5, he talks about not committing murder. However, he said if you are angry with someone, you are equally guilty of murder, a high standard I think we would all agree. This should humble all of us before passing any kind of judgment on others. We have plenty to account for ourselves. Fortunately, we are all offered eternal life through faith in Jesus Christ who died for all our sins as the final atoning sacrifice. That means everyone, no matter what their sin, can receive forgiveness through Jesus.

"I always like to think of a ladder leading up to heaven and visualize where I would be on it in terms of meeting all the laws. None of us would be far up the ladder, no matter what we have done or not done in this life. We can never even come close to being like Jesus, who was without any sin. However, we can strive to be more Christ-like every day. This means we should try to emulate Jesus to others.

"A tough question I ask myself is how do I look to others? Do I emulate Christ-like behavior or not? I have been in conversations where a person will ask me about a professed Christian that behaves very poorly, even on human standards. I then have the exceedingly difficult job of explaining how we are only saved by grace though belief that Jesus Christ is the Son of God. However, unfortunately our behaviors may fall short of what is expected of a follower of Christ.

"So, if people know you are a Christian, you are now an ambassador for Christ, as the Apostle Paul said in 2 Corinthians 5:20. I think it was Francis of Assisi who said, 'Preach the Gospel at all times and when necessary, use words.' This means our actions may be the only Gospel a non-believer sees. At times, our actions do speak louder than our words.

"So, with this background on how to treat those around us, how does this apply to those closest to us? How many of us harbor grudges against friends or family members? Do we not listen before speaking when we should just be quiet? Treating others like Jesus means trying to see the other person's point of view.

"What about marriage? This is something many of us can relate to. I think a lot of the keys to a successful marriage are commitment and compromise. Both parties need to be committed to the relationship which may not always be as smooth as we all would like. I am not saying to stay in an abusive relationship, but apart from that, every effort should be made to stay together.

"There was a reason at the beginning of the relationship why you got married in the first place. This is where forgiveness can go a long way to healing wounds for both sides. The second is compromise. Again, seeing the other's point of view and trying to reach a mutually acceptable solution to a problem is another way of showing each other's love.

"Love is about mutual respect for another person and not getting everything our way every time. If both parties love God, this will draw them closer together. Loving our spouse as ourselves will also ensure each person treats the other like they want to be treated. So, the two greatest commandments Jesus teaches us are directly applicable for a successful marriage. I also believe they are required for successful living.

"I have done a lot of marriage counseling over the years. When I listen to both sides, I realize many times the individuals are just not listening to the other person. They are so wrapped up in their own world that they don't take the time to see the other's point of view. There was a reason the two got married in the first place. Over the years, with added work and family responsibilities, they just forget why they got married. Sometimes the marriage isn't exactly what they thought it would be. News item, nothing in this world is perfect!

"Sometimes I hear one person say their spouse doesn't make them happy. Happiness is a transitory feeling. If you are in a good relationship with God and Jesus, you will experience a joy that lasts a lifetime. It isn't your spouse's job to make you happy. Paul writes in 1 Thessalonians 5:18, 'Give thanks in all circumstances; for this is God's will for you in Christ Jesus.'. So, this is God's command to us to always be thankful, no matter what our situation. I think he is saying God will always be there for us, no matter what happens. And that is something to always be thankful for. So, go find your own joy in life. Don't think it is your spouse's responsibility."

The pastor continued on for a while before he closed with prayer. "Lord, please help all of us to remember the words of your son Jesus that we need to 'Love our neighbor as ourselves' and not be quick to judge others before assessing our own lives and how we all fall short of your perfection. In Jesus' name, we pray, Amen."

FORTY-FOUR

After the service, the two families headed for a local pizzeria that specialized in brick oven baked pizzas and craft beers. The adults were sitting at one table with the kids at an adjacent one.

"So, what did you think about Lakeside Community Church?" Paul asked Chris and Elizabeth.

"It's nothing like I remember as a kid. I can't believe the music and the crowd. There must have been over two thousand people there," Chris replied.

"I loved the music. It really gets everyone in a good mood and excited to be there," Elizabeth added.

"When we first started to attend there, we weren't sure what to make of it all," Linda replied. "We came from a very traditional church setting in Seattle. Some friends we got to know heard we were looking for a church and invited us. I had a similar reaction that you two had. I loved the music but was not sure of the large size and overall format of the service."

"The kids loved the youth group, which sold us at the church. They used to fight us on going to the youth group meetings at our old church. If they're happy going here, hopefully they may still be going to church as adults."

"You put a lot of emphasis on church in your lives," Elizabeth started. "Does it make that much difference for you or your kids?"

"The kids have a lot of influences in their lives every day, and so the messages they get from Lakeside help to counteract these other messages. It's not perfect, but I believe it helps keep them focused on the right things," Linda replied.

"We never put much emphasis on church in our lives. Maybe we should have. I've been genuinely concerned with the direction our two oldest ones are going. However, John did talk with us about his plans this week. It appears your Pastor Jim had some influence on him."

"That's good to hear. I'm not saying a miracle is occurring, but sometimes we all need something to nudge us in a new direction," Paul told them, happy to hear about John. "So, did anything you hear tonight from Pastor John nudge you two at all?"

"It got me thinking about how I tend to stereotype people at times and maybe should listen more before responding," Chris said.

"Now that may be a miracle, you are listening more!" Elizabeth quickly replied. "I probably need to do more of that too. As you both know, Chris and I had a lot of issues leading up to our divorce. Maybe a little more commitment and compromise would have helped, like your pastor recommended."

"Well, it's never too late to fix things," Linda said in a soft voice as she was not sure if she was treading on an extremely sensitive subject area.

"Now that would truly take a miracle to happen. We've been divorced for some time now, and everyone has gotten used to it," Chris said with confidence as he tried to avoid looking at Elizabeth.

"That may be true, but I think we've all been getting along better than expected since you've been back here. We even joked about forgetting the reasons for our divorce." Elizabeth replied, noting how Chris was avoiding making any eye contact with her.

"Well, you never know what the future holds or what God has planned for us," Paul said.

"Now that sounds like what John told me Pastor Jim talked about at the youth group service. He said God has a purpose and plan for each of us," Chris told them.

"That's true. We just may not see it with all the clutter in our daily lives. God may be guiding us somewhere that we don't see right now. You being in Chicago may be for some greater reason than just recovering from surgery," Paul suggested. "It sounds like you're connecting better with your family since you've been back."

"You're right about that. However, we'll have to see how that holds when I'm back in Los Angeles in a couple of weeks." Looking at his watch, Chris said, "Hey, it's getting late, and we should go. Thanks again for a great evening. It looks like the kids are getting along well too."

"So, what did you think about the service tonight?" Jessica asked the Baldwin children.

"It was different than I expected. The music was opposite of what I remember when going to church services occasionally in the past," Sarah replied.

"The pastor talked about not judging others. This reminded me of talking with my friend Bob a couple of days ago. He really dissed Christians. He said they look down on non-Christians and try to get people when they have a lot of problems, like what Emma talked about her father being killed in a car accident. Bob said Christians use that to get people interested," John added.

"Yea, my friend Amy made jokes about Christians getting married real young and women having lots of kids and having no careers," Sarah jumped into the conversation.

"That's not true. Christians get stereotyped all the time by non-believers. We aren't perfect either and that's why Jesus told us not to judge others. We have enough to deal with ourselves," Michael pushed back with an almost angry tone. This reminded him of comments he had heard from other kids at school or on his soccer team.

"So, who's really judging others, us or them?" Jessica asked.

"When I started to get interested in going to church, some of my friends also warned me about how judgmental and boring Christians are," Jennifer added. "I guess I was not sure if that was true, but I knew Jessica was not judging or boring to hang out with. So, I thought I'd try it out."

"If being boring means not partying or drinking until we are drunk or sick, I guess that's OK with me," Michael said. "I do get a lot of pressure to do that kind of stuff. Some of the kids try to get me interested in drugs. I think they're all trying to escape from stuff they can't handle. I think Jesus understands this and told us to let Him take care of our problems and to trust Him."

"As you probably know, I do hang out with kids that party and drink a lot," John began. "I have a good time with them, but I'm not sure that's what I should be doing. Michael, you may be right, I do that to feel good maybe because I've been feeling bad about a lot of stuff at my home. I don't talk about it much, but the divorce really got to me," John said in a low somber voice, so his parents didn't overhear him. Also, he felt almost like a major realization was hitting him about himself.

"While we are confessing our real feelings, I also have to say I've been going through a lot of tough stuff. I think only Jennifer had the guts to admit it and do something constructive about it,' Sarah said also in a low tone of voice.

"Wow! I thought I was the only one who felt so bad about what was happening with our family. Why didn't you all talk about it?" Jennifer blurted out.

"I didn't want to seem not cool about things. Some of my friends have divorced parents, and they act like everything is fine. I just wanted to fit in," John told the group.

"Me too; I thought I would be an outcast with my friends if I got depressed about things. It seems like having divorced parents is almost as normal as any other family," Sarah added.

"That's what I found at Lakeside. There are a lot of kids like us who have family problems and have trouble dealing with them. Some have divorced parents or other problems. They made me feel normal about my feelings. They also showed me how Jesus could relate to their problems. I never thought about Jesus understanding my problems," Jennifer told them with a sound of relief in her voice that she was not the only one in her family upset about things.

"That's why I invited you to visit our youth group. I knew you'd see that you aren't alone with having problems," Jessica said amazed at how inviting Jennifer to her church changed Jennifer's life.

"Well, maybe I'll consider coming back to the youth group again. It may help me deal with some things," John said as he started to see his situation differently.

"Maybe you can see Emma more," Jennifer teased him.

"Well, that would be good also!" John laughed. Although he found Emma physically attractive, her story was even more attractive to him.

"So how about you, Sarah? Would you consider going back?" Michael asked with a slight smile.

"I guess so. My approach doesn't seem to be working very well," she said as she wondered if Michael may be interested in seeing her again also.

"Great, it will be nice getting together again like we used to!" Jessica exclaimed in an optimistic tone.

"It's like the old days again. You know we all really missed you, and it's been great seeing you here again." Linda said. She hugged Chris and Elizabeth as they got up to leave with the kids.

The kids asked about staying longer, which surprised all the adults. After some arguments, they got up and headed outside.

FORTY-FIVE

What do you think about our conversation with Paul and Linda?" Elizabeth asked Chris after they got back home, and the kids headed into the basement to watch a movie.

"It was OK. What are you getting at?"

"I couldn't help but notice you avoided eye contact with me when talking about our divorce and getting back together."

"That was a sensitive topic for me, and they caught me off guard."

"Things have been going well here. I think the kids are doing much better."

"Is that enough to consider getting back together?"

"Well, it's a start."

"I don't know. Maybe it was a bad idea for me to stay here."

"Why, because you may remember some of the good things we had here? Or do you miss Candy?"

"That's Candace. To tell you the truth, I don't know where that relationship is going. Also, my promotion may not happen. Apparently, the management thought Joe did a great job in my absence. There's just too much on my mind right now."

"Look, let's both get a good night's rest and leave all this alone," Elizabeth said as she saw the anxiety building in Chris. She was also surprised he shared his thoughts on his relationship with Candace. She realized she too needed some time to consider what was said tonight with a clearer mind.

"Tonight, wasn't as bad as I thought it would be," John told Sarah and Jennifer as they were watching a movie in the basement.

"That service was totally different than how I remember church," Sarah replied. "It took a while but I kind of liked the music and light show, although it didn't seem very religious to me."

"It doesn't matter what the service looks like if it is praising God. A lot of people think the music must be very boring to be in a worship service," Jennifer told them.

"I got to admit, the pastor's message was interesting, and I didn't notice it went on for about forty-five minutes!" John told Jennifer as he reached for more popcorn.

"I told you the messages were interesting. I had fun at dinner afterwards. It was nice having the whole family together," Jennifer added.

"You know, I did have a good time. Michael isn't that much of a nerd. We talked about a lot of stuff. I think he even noticed you, Sarah," John said as he tried to get a reaction from her.

"I don't know. I kind of like him, but some of my friends think he's boring."

"What do you care what your friends think? If you like him, that's all that matters," John told her as he realized this was the second time he was defending Michael. "Maybe you should ask him if he would like to go to a movie or something with you."

"Isn't that kind of awkward for a girl to ask a guy out on a date?"

"Well, one of you has to, if you're ever going to go out on a date," Jennifer exclaimed. "I think you're making too big a deal out of the whole thing. Maybe I can talk to Jessica and see if she can get Michael to ask you out?"

"I can't believe I'm agreeing to this and having my little sister help me go out with a guy, but that works for me."

"Great, I'll talk to her about it next time I see her."

"You know, it was kind of fun hanging out with Michael and Jessica," John began sharing. "I remember we used to hang out together when we first moved here. Michael and I even played soccer together on the same youth soccer team. I don't know what happened. I used to like playing sports, but as I got older, I lost interest, especially after Mom and Dad got divorced," John said as he thought about the way things were years back.

"Have you guys noticed that Mom and Dad seem to be getting along better?" Sarah asked them.

"Yes, I think Dad is interested in what we're doing too. I don't think he was that interested when they were married," John added.

"Do you think they'll get back together?" Jennifer asked hopefully.

"No way. Dad still talks about his job and possible big promotion. I know he keeps in touch with his girlfriend Candy, too. I sometimes hear him talking with her at night."

"I think her name is Candace, not Candy," Sarah said but wondered why she was correcting John.

"Well, that's what Mom calls her. I don't think she likes her very much, even though she's never met her."

"I don't think I like her either. She may be our stepmom if you can believe that."

"That would be weird," Sarah told them, realizing she hadn't really thought about that possibility before.

"I think Dad's leaving next week to head back to LA, and then everything will go back to the way it was before he got here," John told them, as he tried to stop the discussion about Candace.

"I'm going to miss seeing him every day," Jennifer said in a quiet, sad tone.

"I'm sure he'll call us a lot," Sarah told Jennifer as she tried to cheer her up, although she doubted that would happen.

"I've liked talking with him about what I will do after high school," John said.

"It's been nice having him around the last few weeks. I wasn't happy about him coming here when Mom first told us."

"Me neither. I guess I was mad about everything and blamed him," Sarah told them.

"I think they may still get back together," Jennifer declared confidently as they all sat in silence watching the rest of the movie and thought about what their father being home the past six weeks meant to them.

FORTY-SIX

So how was your weekend?" Samantha asked Elizabeth at lunch on Monday after the weekend service she attended.

"It went well. My family went to a Saturday service with our old friends Paul and Linda Chambers and their kids. It was nice doing something normal as a complete family. I almost forgot I was divorced. Chris and I were talking with the Chambers like old times. Our kids also seem to be getting along well. John and Sarah had drifted apart from Michael and Jessica Chambers over the past few years. I hope they stay connected. I think the Chambers kids can have a better influence on mine than their current friends."

"That sounds encouraging. What about you and Chris? What do you think will happen after he leaves?" Samantha asked cautiously.

"I don't know. To be honest, we seem to be getting along well lately, like nothing ever happened."

"Would you consider getting married again?"

"Maybe, who knows?"

"What about his job and girlfriend?

"He could always get a job in Chicago, although he seems

really focused on this big promotion. Also, I think he may have gotten serious with Candace. I can't believe I didn't call her Candy! I guess a lot has changed over the past six weeks."

"From what I have seen of guys, they can't help being attracted to younger women. Women our age just can't complete."

"I won't compete with any woman. This is about Chris and me. At any rate, it would take a miracle for us to get back together. Too much has happened since our divorce. Besides, I think Chris has moved on with his job and girlfriend. I just must learn to accept that and move on also. I'm not sure why I let him stay with us. Perhaps, I let him stay here, hoping something might change. I don't know. He'll be heading back to Los Angeles this week, and we'll all go back to the way things have been. I'm sure his visit with us will be long forgotten soon enough."

FORTY-SEVEN

So, this is the big week. How are you doing?" Elizabeth asked Chris in the kitchen.

"Pretty good, I'm eating reasonably and not getting constipated! I guess I can get off the stool softeners. As you know, the doctor has cleared me to go back to work with no restrictions. He told me my abdomen muscles were about 97% of full strength prior to surgery. It will take about a year for the complete healing, but I won't notice it.

"I wish I could say the same about my job. My friend Sam told me that my temporary replacement, Joe, has done a great job and may get my promotion. I worked so hard for that, and then this surgery happened. I just don't get it. Everything was going great and then out of nowhere, I'm taken out of the game."

"Maybe this all happened for some reason we don't understand. I think your presence here has had a beneficial effect on the kids. They may not admit it, but I believe they've been happier having you around."

"You think so? I've been a lousy dad for a long time."

"Also, there is Candace back in LA," Elizabeth said, not sure if she wanted to bring up that subject.

"Finally, you call her Candace! Wow, you really got right to the point. I don't know. You and I seem to be getting along much better. I wonder if that is more due to the novelty of me being here, or is there something long-term going on between us?" Chris replied with a deep sense of sincerity in his voice.

"I know what you mean. This whole thing is so weird. I never thought we would even be talking about this after the divorce was over. I wonder how this all came to be. It seems like impossible odds."

"Have you been praying about all this?" Chris asked, not sure if he believed in prayer or God.

"Yes, I have been, every day. Linda has been very encouraging. She seems so at peace sometimes. She told me it's because she has learned to trust God and not try to control the things that happen herself."

"I really don't know what to make of prayer or God. He seems remote to me if He exists at all."

"Well, I can't help but wonder if all that has happened to us these past six weeks is not part of a grander plan of God for us. What about your job?"

"I'll stop in to see the president, Don, when I get back to talk about all I've done for the company and how I laid the groundwork for Joe's so-called success. If I don't get the promotion, I can always look for another job, if I want. LA is a big city."

"Maybe you could look for a job in Chicago. It's also a big city," Elizabeth suggested.

"I don't know. Maybe I should pray about it?" Chris asked sarcastically. "I really need to think about a lot of things."

After Linda left to do some errands, Chris decided to call Candace.

"Hey there. How are things going?" Chris started the conversation, not sure where it would go.

"Great. So, it has been six weeks. Are you ready to get back here? I have all kinds of plans for us to catch up," Candace said very excitedly. "I can't believe how much I missed you."

"Me too. It seems like it's been a long time. It has been nice seeing Chicago again and my kids. I think my visit here has been helpful. The older ones, John, and Sarah were getting into some problems, and they seem to be turning things around. Jennifer seems to be doing well, with or without me."

"That sounds good. You probably won't have to see them again for a while after you get back here."

"Well, I think I need to keep more in touch with them."

"OK, I guess a visit a couple times a year wouldn't hurt," Candace said with resignation in her voice.

"We can talk about this when I get back," Chris said, not wanting to get into an argument with her on the phone.

"When will you be leaving Chicago?"

"I should be leaving in a couple of days. My old neighbors, Paul and Linda Chambers, want our family to come over for dinner. Sort of a farewell thing."

"We'll have a welcome home party for you when you get back here."

"That sounds great," Chris said, not sure where exactly home was anymore.

"Some friends are here that I promised to go shopping with today, so I got to go. Love you and look forward to seeing you soon," Candace said as she heard the doorbell ring.

"Me too, have a good time with your friends," Chris said as he ended the call with her.

The next evening, Chris, Elizabeth, and their children

went over to the Chambers home for dinner together before Chris left.

"It's great to see you all again," Linda said as she greeted them at the front door. "Come on in. There's some time before dinner so you kids can head into the family room or the basement to hang out or play some video games. The 'old folks' can settle down in the living room for a while."

"That sounds good to me," Chris said, not sure of what to expect in the conversation.

"So, how are you doing?" Paul asked after each couple made themselves comfortable on two couches in the living room.

"I'm doing well," Chris began. "My surgeon told me I can resume normal activities, like lifting more than ten pounds, although it's not like I do power lifting! More noticeable is that I'm back to a normal diet. I think I even gained a couple of pounds. If I'm not careful, I'll be back to more than my pre-surgery weight before I know it. I could stand to keep a few pounds off," Chris said with a laugh.

"Elizabeth told me she thought you look even better since your surgery," Linda said slyly as she looked toward Elizabeth, who was embarrassed.

"So is that what she told you? You never mentioned that to me," he said as he looked at Elizabeth with a big smile.

"I didn't because I knew I would never hear the end of it," she replied, trying to avoid eye contact with Chris.

"I probably shouldn't have said anything," Linda said apologetically to Linda.

"That's OK. I guess there are still no secrets between Chris and me," she said with a laugh. She was happy Linda mentioned it, although she would never have had the courage because she was not sure where that comment might lead. Somehow, she was sure Linda knew that too.

"How are things going at work while you've been away?" Paul asked, as he thought this was a good time to change the subject.

"I don't know. My friend Sam told me my sub has done a great job, and I may be competing with him for the executive vice-president job. I can't believe that, after all the work I put into getting things set up for the major deal with the Europeans."

"I'm sure management knows about all the work you put into getting things set up. You can't control what happens in life. This is especially true when it comes to our health. I have outlived a few people over the years, forget about having to take time off for health problems. Life is short, and we all need to enjoy each day. I've known a lot of people who worry too much about tomorrow and don't enjoy being here today."

"Well, I may need to think about your advice. I worry too much about the future. That's one thing being out of work for several weeks has taught me. I was forced to slow down and just focus on the present. I do feel like I've gotten a new lease on life. Who knows what would have happened if I decided to wait another year for my colonoscopy. My doctor said you never know what may become of polyps."

"I think your relationship with the kids has improved tremendously," Elizabeth said, using Chris' comments as an opening to encourage him to stay in touch with the family. "You have great conversations with each of them. Please remember that when you're back in LA and call regularly. A visit to Chicago occasionally would be nice too."

"I think our kids are also reconnecting. They seem to be getting along well," Linda added.

"John seems to be getting interested in school again and even goes to watch some of Michael's soccer games," Elizabeth told them with a hint of amazement in her voice.

"It really has been nice having the two families together again these past weeks. We should commit to getting together when Chris is in town. Also, Elizabeth, let's continue meeting for coffee regularly late in the afternoon. I enjoy our discussions," Linda told Chris and Elizabeth, hoping they would eventually get back together in the future.

"I've enjoyed our discussions and sharing about things," Elizabeth replied.

"I also have enjoyed being back in the neighborhood," Chris said. "I don't know any of my neighbors in Valencia. I just go to work and come home to eat and sleep and repeat the process every day. This has reminded me about how such good friends you've been over the years. That really means a lot to me and Elizabeth, if I can speak for her."

"You certainly can about Paul and Linda," Elizabeth said.

"Why don't you help me get the grill going, and we can let Linda and Elizabeth talk about us while we are gone," Paul suggested to Chris as he laughed at his own joke.

Paul and Chris left for the backyard while Linda and Elizabeth continued the discussion of how things had been going since Chris had been at her home.

"I got to tell you, that I'm actually glad you told Chris about my comments on how he looks since his surgery."

"I kind of thought you would be OK with it. I guess we know each other too well! So, what's going to happen between you and Chris?"

"Nothing. He's getting ready to go back to his job in LA and his girlfriend Candy, or I should call her Candace."

"And that's it? Have you discussed how you feel about him and your marriage?"

"Well, indirectly. He also has shared some uncertainty about his relationship with Candace. Look, I can't compete with some woman half my age and certainly more fun to be around. I'm just a boring middle-aged woman with three kids. I'm sure Chris looks forward to being able to pretend we don't exist when he's in Los Angeles."

"I wouldn't be too sure of that. That might have been true in the past, but I think he has reconsidered after being here for six weeks. You said he's getting along better with his children, and I think you and he are enjoying being together."

"That's true, but after so much has happened, I find it hard to believe things can be changed."

"Have you been praying about this regularly?"

"Yes, I have, but I don't expect a miracle."

"But God can supply just such a miracle in His time, not ours. You may need to be patient and just keep praying."

"I guess I can keep doing that."

"That's all you can do. Now let's check up on the guys before they burn dinner," Linda said, thinking she had made her point and prayed also for God to step into the situation and intercede.

The next day while Chris was in the family room watching a cable news program, the front doorbell rang.

"I wonder who is at the door in the middle of the day," Chris wondered to himself as he was starting to think about heading back to Los Angeles later this week.

"Hi Pastor Jim, I didn't expect to see you again," Chris said with surprise in his voice.

"I was talking to Jennifer after our last weekend youth service, and she told me you would be heading back to Los Angeles this week."

"Yea, sure, I'm starting to think about it. Please come in."

"So, how are you feeling?"

"Great. To tell you the truth, I could have gone back last week, except my diet was still a little tough. I can now eat pretty much anything along with reasonable portions."

"Are there any other reasons that may have delayed your return?" Pastor Jim asked as he sensed something deeper going on. After years of counseling people, he had developed an intuition about sensing hidden stories.

"What do you mean?"

"When counseling people, I've found that many times what people say is not the real issue on their mind."

"Is this a counseling session?"

"No, but your daughter seemed concerned about your leaving. She shared with me that it has been great having you around."

"Really? I have trouble figuring out what my kids think about anything these days."

"She asked me to stop by and talk with you about your leaving, although I'm not sure what it is I am to talk about. Sometimes I believe that's how the Holy Spirit works. I'm placed in a situation by God and trust He will guide me."

"What do you mean by that?"

"God sometimes places us in situations that we don't understand to serve His purpose."

"That sounds a little like my being here in Chicago. I never figured this happening. I sometimes wonder why I'm here and why this happened to me. To make matters more complicated, I'm not sure I do want to go back to Los Angeles. I haven't told anyone here that yet."

"That's kind of how things work at times. One of my favorite Bible verses is 2 Corinthians, 4:18, 'So we fix our eyes not on what is seen, but on what is unseen, since what is seen is temporary, but what is unseen is eternal'"

"What is that all about?"

"What it says is that what we see around us down here on earth is part of a much grander plan of God's in heaven. We may not always see it, but we need to trust that God is in control and knows what's best for us."

"So, God caused my need for surgery?"

"Probably not, but He will use situations for a greater good. In your case, this time in Chicago might have been used for you to see your family in a different light than how you saw them in Los Angeles. So, while you're focusing on recovery, God has been working His plans for you."

"I am not much of a churchgoing person, but I tend to agree with you that I have been seeing my family and my ex-wife differently. What did you say about forty days when I was in the hospital before my surgery?"

"I gave you a few examples of how God changed people's lives in forty days. I believe you've been here about that long now."

"Just about forty days. If you promise not to discuss this with anyone, I'd like to tell you what's been happening over these forty or so days."

"No problem. I can be very discreet," Pastor Jim said with a smile, thinking he'd heard it all over the years.

"Let me start with my kids. I'm talking with them much better than before my divorce. My oldest, John, is even asking me for advice on what to do after graduating from high school. I think my oldest daughter, Sarah, is starting to hang out with a better crowd and focusing on school more. She may even like going to your youth group services."

"Well, that may be true; I think she also likes Michael Chambers. But like I said, God uses all situations to serve His purposes," Pastor Jim said jokingly.

"But here's the strangest thing, Elizabeth and I are getting along better with each passing week. At first, things were cold, which I couldn't blame her for. But now, we spend a few hours each evening just talking about things like work or the kids. We even look at each other like we haven't since maybe we were dating. We joke about forgetting why we even got divorced."

"What about Candace?"

"Thank God you didn't say Candy! I don't know. As I look at our relationship from literally a distance, I'm not sure why I even started dating her. She's extremely attractive and fun to be with, but after that, our relationship is shallow, at best. I think she represents all the things I felt I was missing in my marriage. It wasn't just good times all the time as our marriage continued and the kids got older."

"As a Christian, I would tell you that Satan used your thoughts about your marriage to drive you and your wife apart. Jesus said in John 10, 'The thief comes only to kill and steal and destroy; I have come that they may have life and have it to the full.' We need to be constantly aware of Satan looking at opportunities to take our focus from God and Christ."

"I'm not sure I get all that you just said. Neither Elizabeth nor I have been in church much since we were kids. However, I admit, I let my fantasy of what a marriage should be contribute to the divorce. Maybe there's something to God working in the background up there affecting things down here. I'm not sure how else I would explain it."

"I have found that keeping the focus on God tends to help me stay on the right track. We all need that at times. That is what going to worship services on the weekends is all about. It gets us refocused on God for the week ahead. So, what are you thinking about doing?"

"I'm afraid to even say it aloud. I'm thinking about quitting my job, breaking up with Candace, and staying here in Chicago. Maybe I can get my marriage and family back where it should be."

"What's stopping you from doing that?"

"Fear. Plain and simple fear. I have a good job and a gorgeous girlfriend who is fun to be with. But the most I fear is being rejected by my kids and Elizabeth. So much has happened, I don't know if it's too late to go back to the way things were."

"I don't believe it's ever too late to correct a wrong. Although things may not be the same as before, they may be better. Everyone will have learned from this experience."

"I don't know if I can make this major change in my life."

"Let me tell you my life verse."

"What's a life verse?"

"It's a verse in scripture that really captures my attention and is one that can help me get through all situations. For me it is Joshua 1:9, 'Be strong and courageous. Do not be afraid; do not be discouraged, for the LORD your God will be with you wherever you go.' This was God's promise to Joshua as he was taking over the leadership of the Jewish people after Moses died. This is also God's promise for us."

"Well, I know what I have to do. Thanks, Pastor, for stopping by. I'll keep you posted," Chris said as Pastor Jim went to the front door.

Pastor Jim left, wondering which path Chris was going to choose at this crossroads in his life.

FORTY-EIGHT

There was whispering among the crowd as they awaited the start of the service. As the senior pastor stood up and approached the podium, a hush fell over the crowd.

"I want to thank everyone here today who have come to remember Christopher Baldwin," said Pastor Jim Stone, senior pastor of Lakeside Community Church as he began the service. "I've known Chris for about forty years. I was a youth pastor in the days that I met him. I must say, he had a remarkable life. Chris was not much of a believer when I met him, and he was difficult to reach with any discussion of God or Jesus. What you will hear today, however, is a testament to how what is impossible for man is possible for God.

"Some of you here may not know how I got to know Chris. Others that do, please bear with me. I love to tell this story. I first met Chris at the request of his daughter Jennifer. She was a member of the youth group and her dad, Chris, was going to have surgery to remove what would be a large benign polyp from his colon. Her parents were divorced, and Chris lived in Los Angeles. However, he was going to need help after the surgery and he stayed with his ex-wife, Elizabeth, and their three children for six weeks. I told him that God has used forty days or about six weeks to change lives as discussed in the scriptures. I don't think he took much stock in it, but he was always very polite with me.

"As a pastor, I get used to people not blowing me off directly but being nice to me! Near the time he was about to leave, we spoke about things. I don't remember the details, but I'll never forget how he left me hanging about what he would do. I had asked him if he would stay in Chicago and try to rebuild his marriage or go back to his girlfriend in Los Angeles. All he said was, 'I know what I am going to do' and showed me to the door.

"So, there I am walking out of the door, not knowing what he would do. I did believe that the Holy Spirit was talking to him, even if he didn't know it yet. However, God gives us all the gift of free will. We can do what we want, even if it may not be what God wants for us. I could tell the whole story, but there are several people here that can tell it better than I.

"First, I introduce his wife, Elizabeth," Pastor Jim said as he extended his hand in her direction and sat down in a chair on the stage.

An elderly woman slowly got up from her chair and approached the podium to address the crowd that had gathered to honor her husband. She was extremely nervous, not used to speaking to such a large audience. However, she reminded herself these were friends that she and Chris had known over a lifetime, and they were only here to support her and her family.

As she got to the podium, she steadied herself. She had developed balance problems as she had gotten older and was careful to keep herself stable.

She had a couple of pages of notes to refer to. After she looked down at the notes, she looked up out over the crowd gathered before her. As she looked over the room, there were many familiar faces. A few smiled at her as she made eye contact with them. Although she was very sorrowful, she was also very thankful for all the years she had with Chris. She smiled as she began to speak.

"I want to thank everyone for coming today to honor and remember Chris. There was a time I never would have thought this would happen. As Pastor Jim said, we were divorced and lived in separate cities. Chris ignored me and worse yet, our children. Don't get me wrong, it took two of us to get married and again took two of us to get divorced. Although I blamed him for all our problems, as time went by, I realized I was as much at fault as he was. We lost our focus on each other and our family.

"But worse, we never had a focus on God. I heard it said that if a couple puts God first above even themselves, they will both be drawn together to God and therefore to each other. The pastor at our first wedding said it's like God is the apex of a triangle, and the two people are at the other points. Both merge towards God. Now I haven't realized this for some time. However, I thank God for some friends who helped me get my focus on God.

"As you heard, Chris needed some help after his surgery, and his girlfriend in LA wasn't up to the task. You know she was about half his age. I think they used to call that an upgrade from me, his older ex-wife and mother of his children. He wanted to be free from the responsibilities associated with being married. I must admit, I was, at the time, jealous of his freedom. I had to take care of the kids and keep a job and house going. So, he called unexpectedly and asked to stay with us for a while. I almost refused, but thank God, I didn't. At the time, I didn't know why I agreed to have him stay. I now believe I got a very slight nudge from God to let him back into my life, at least for about forty days."

She paused for a long time. Some people in the audience started to whisper to each other, not sure what she was going to say or if she was too overcome with emotion to continue. Pastor Jim was wondering if he should get up to help her. Then her voice rose as she continued.

"Forty days! That led to forty more years of marriage, which led to his having forty years of relationships with his children, and then many years with his grandchildren, and yes, a few great-grandchildren. This would have never happened if I hadn't opened my house and my life to him for just a little while. I had no idea that I would be standing here today telling you about how God changed our lives and our children's lives.

"Chris went back to Los Angeles after six weeks as planned. Even though we seemed to be getting a little closer over the time he was here, he still went back without saying much about what had happened while he was with us. So, I just figured, nothing appeared to have changed, and we would hardly hear from him again. As expected, several months went by with only a few phone calls from him. One day, the doorbell rang, and there he was at the door. I asked if he needed my help again. He said what he wanted was another chance at our marriage.

"I asked about his job. He said that he got the promotion to executive vice president but decided to leave the company. He already had a job in Chicago at the company he used to work for.

"I asked about his girlfriend, Candy, or I should say Candace. He said he ended the relationship. He also had rented a place in the same town we lived in so he could be closer to the kids.

"He had left behind everything to take a chance on our marriage. I really didn't know what to say to him. I did say that I was open to trying to make it work. I asked him what changed his mind about our marriage and family. He didn't know, but something kept telling him he should go back to Chicago, and maybe it was God. Years later he would say he believed the Holy Spirit worked through several people to get him to think about reconsidering our marriage. The visit with Pastor Jim and conversations with our friends Paul and Linda Chambers had more impact on him than he had thought.

"We started dating again like when we were in college. Even the kids used to joke about us being like high school kids. At the same time, we started to go to Lakeside Community Church with our whole family. Paul and Linda were great and helped us along with our faith journey."

At this point, Elizabeth looked out into the audience and saw Paul and Linda Chambers in the front row of seats. She paused to acknowledge them with a smile and nod of her head. They returned the smile as they seemed to collectively read each other's minds about those days so long ago.

"Eventually, Chris and I were baptized here, right on this stage in the pool that is below it. Even though we were baptized as infants, we felt we wanted to show our renewed dedication to Christ by being baptized again. We also remarried in this church by, who else, but Pastor Jim presiding. Our children also responded, and Chris developed great relationships with each of them, I found my relationships with our children got stronger too. Part of it was sharing all the responsibilities with Chris and not carrying the 'weight of the world' by myself.

"One challenge for me was to forgive Chris and myself. I

was truly angry with him and jealous of his relationship with Candace. Even though we were divorced, and he had every right to date whoever he wanted, I still felt betrayed in some odd sense. So, I prayed to God about finding it in my heart to forgive myself for feeling that way and able to put aside what was in the past and just look forward to the future in our renewed relationship. Over time this did happen and much more as you will hear today.

"I believe that Chris' need for surgery was used by God to place him back into our lives long enough for the Holy Spirit to touch him and me. I genuinely believe our remarriage and bringing the family back together was a miracle. I could go on and on about Chris and the changes in our lives, but I think our children can tell their own stories about their father. I will let our oldest, John, tell his story now."

As his mother moved slowly from the podium, a middle-aged man stood up and helped her to her seat. He then walked to the podium. He looked out over the auditorium and saw some familiar and many unfamiliar faces. John thought how many people were touched by his father's life. He thought about where he would have been today if it wasn't for his dad. There was a time when he wouldn't have thought his father would ever be a part of his life again. But here he was about to give a eulogy for him.

"For those that don't know me I am John, my dad's oldest son. The divorce was extremely hard for me, although I didn't talk much about it. I suppose Mom thought I was doing fine, but I wasn't. I lost interest in sports that I used to play and school. Then Dad left for Los Angeles. I had no interest in my future. I drank a lot and even tried drugs a few times. After a while I realized Mom knew what was going on, but she was too overwhelmed with life to talk with me about it. I took advantage of that and started a downward spiral.

"Even with my parents not being together, having my dad in the area to see regularly was more important than I had thought. I only came to realize that after he came back and eventually remarried Mom. I was old enough to know about his life in LA, including his girlfriend. Thinking of him starting a new life had bothered me. I really felt like I was abandoned for good.

"When he came to stay with us for a while, I thought this was only temporary, and I would just tolerate him. I came to at least not like him, if not hate him for everything that happened to our family. At first, we got into some arguments about my friends and not doing much in school. I thought he was just pretending to be a father while he was with us. However, towards the end of his visit, I sensed a genuine concern starting to develop. I even had trouble staying mad at him, although I did try," John chuckled at this as did many in the audience.

He continued, "After he left, I thought I must have been imagining the changes and now I was back to reality. So, you can imagine my surprise when he showed up months later. I wasn't sure how it would go, but I decided to give him a chance. We would get together on weekends to talk about things, and he'd tell me how he wanted to be a real father to me, Sarah, and Jennifer.

"After Mom and Dad got married again, I finally felt this was for real. I opened up to him and Mom about my feelings concerning the divorce and how I really needed their help in moving forward with a plan. I decided to intern at my neighbor Dr. Chambers' engineering company for a summer. He offered me that opportunity in my junior year, and I'm glad I took it. I decided to study engineering in college, eventually getting a master's degree. I have a great family and kids and have enjoyed a life I may not have had if God had not stepped into our lives and had my father stay with us."

Paul Chambers smiled and nodded as John looked over to him and Linda. Even at his advanced years, he thought how God never ceased to amaze him with how He can change lives.

"That's the other thing, after my parents started attending church and got baptized, I began thinking that there may be something to God and Jesus. So, I started attending the youth group. Pastor Jim can be very persuasive! As you probably already guessed, I also accepted Jesus as my Lord and Savior and was baptized. I can't believe how much Christ has done in my life and my family's life. I agree with my mom about my wife and I putting God first in our lives, which has always drawn us closer to each other.

"It scares me when I think about what could have easily been my life if my dad had not come to stay with us. The scriptures say that God works all things for good for those who love him, and I honestly believe that.

"I also want to thank everyone for coming today. Although I am saddened with my father's death, I have the Christian hope of being with him again and that is a reason to celebrate. By that I mean not only celebrating and praising God for what He did in our lives but also celebrate what Jesus has done for all our lives.

"I think I've talked long enough. I'll turn things over to my sister Sarah."

John turned and started to walk back to his seat on the stage. He looked at the casket for a few seconds and fought back a tear. He looked past the casket and saw the baptismal pool in the back of the stage. It was covered unless baptisms were planned for the weekend services. He remembered being baptized so many years ago. He still was learning what it meant to be a follower of Christ. Trusting in God at these times was particularly challenging. John hugged his sister as she passed by him on her way to the podium. And John gave his mother a hug before sitting down.

Sarah approached the podium a little nervous about speaking to such a large audience. She was thinking about what she was going to say and how there was a time that she could not imagine such an ending to her father's life.

"Like my mom and brother, I also want to thank you all for coming today to honor my father, Christopher Baldwin. Growing up, for a while I guess I lived the classic upper middle-class life as a kid. We went on great vacations and got pretty much everything I wanted for Christmas or, for that matter, any time of the year. I didn't really think about it at the time, but there wasn't much I felt deprived of. Then, what seemed to be out of nowhere, my parents sat us down at the kitchen table one evening and said they were getting divorced. I didn't know how to respond. I wanted to cry but didn't until I was back in my bedroom. I thought it was somehow my fault. I thought about how many of my friends' parents were divorced. I never thought I'd be in the same situation. But there I was, in the same situation.

"After the divorce was completed, things changed. For a while, Dad would visit us regularly, and we'd stay at his place on alternating weekends, the typical divorced family lifestyle. Then Dad got a new job in Los Angeles and moved there. We didn't hear from him much, and mom seemed overwhelmed with things. I started to hang out with kids that weren't the best for me. They offered me an escape from my home life, although I didn't think about it that way at the time.

"Again, out of nowhere, my father was back in our house recovering from surgery. He started to get interested in my life and even talked to me about some of the choices I was making. At first, I thought he was just bored and trying to hassle me. But as time went by, I came to believe he was genuinely interested in what I was doing. When I thought we were really starting to connect, he left again. I wondered if I would see him again. I even prayed about it! I attended a few sessions of the youth group at this church, and one of the kids prayed with me about it. I wasn't sure about that but thought it wouldn't hurt, so I prayed about it on my own. To my surprise, my father showed up several months later here in Chicago.

"We started spending a lot of time together and talking about things. He said that he had been trying to escape from life in Los Angeles. I suddenly realized that was what I was doing with my friends. Well, after my parents remarried, it was like life suddenly changed. I discovered that being a family was much more important than getting all the material things I wanted. This became a model for me as I grew up. I wanted that same kind of family life that my parents finally had. I also gave my life to Christ and got baptized, although that part took many years. In fact, I met a great guy in college who encouraged me to take that next step.

"Since then, we married, and we've been blessed with three great kids. Yes, we probably give them too much at times, which my father would point out from time to time. You see, he finally stopped chasing after better paying jobs and promotions and focused on family and God. These are the things that have eternal value. He taught me and my siblings that. However, I believe my little sister, Jennifer, already discovered this truth as a young girl. She helped the rest of us to learn this. But I'll let her tell you that part of the story."

Sarah turned and saw her family, not broken as it was so many years ago. She smiled at them, and they smiled back at her. They were a living miracle every day to her. She had given up on this ever happening, but she thought, *God never gave up on them.*

Jennifer rose and hugged Sarah as they passed each other in front of their father's casket. As she approached the podium, she thought back to the many years she had been in the audience singing along with the worship team with guitars playing very loud, light shows, and some smoke that created a very uplifting experience. Then the pastor would deliver the teaching from the same place where she was standing, looking out at the audience who were partially hidden in the darkened auditorium with most of the lighting on the stage.

"Like the others, thanks to you all for coming today. I think you heard enough about my father leaving, coming back, leaving, and coming back for good!" she said with a small laugh and smile. There were a few chuckles from the audience.

"So, let me tell you about life after my parents remarried. The first thing we did was we took a vacation to spend some time together and get to know each other again. Our neighbors, the Chambers, suggested Kiawah Island near Charleston, South Carolina. It was great; we spent two weeks in a villa. We spent the days on the beach or bike riding along trails. Dad and John would golf a few rounds while we were there. At night, we cooked dinner together. This was so great; we really got a chance to spend time talking with each other while cooking and eating dinner. After dinner, we'd go get ice cream at a place called Scoopers. We really connected again as a family. All the bad times seemed like a distant memory. We never looked back, only forward.

"I spent some time telling this story because we adopted Kiawah as a place where our family would get together for many years to come. As we got married and had children, we continued the tradition with our growing families. Mom and Dad really enjoyed seeing everyone together. I realized that these great family memories were truly a miracle from God. He somehow stepped into our lives and used my father's surgery to do more than just heal him physically; he healed him and the rest of us spiritually.

"After my parents were divorced, my friend, Jessica Chambers, who is here today, invited me to her church youth group. At that time, Pastor Jim was the youth pastor. I spent some time talking with him and Jessica about my feelings of sadness and helplessness. This is when I was told about Jesus Christ and how He died for all our sins. I learned that He also experienced the same feelings I had during His life on earth. I remember the story of how Jesus wept when He heard His friend Lazarus had died. I found that awesome that the Son of God could care that much for a person that He would cry.

"Over time, I became a believer and got baptized here. This helped me cope with my family situation. I then started to talk with my siblings and parents about God and Jesus. I admit this was a hard sell. However, I believe the Holy Spirit worked on us all through that time.

"I was so moved by what God did for my family, I spent several years as a missionary after graduating from college. I felt like I had to help others as God did me and my family. There are so many needs out there that I sometimes found it hard to believe that one person, like me, could make much of a difference. But I think the next person to speak will be a great witness to the power of God working through one person."

As Jennifer left the podium to sit down, a family friend stood up and gave Jennifer a hug as she went to her chair. She was an older woman in her mid-sixties, well dressed and could pass for a woman twenty years younger. She went ahead to hug Sarah and John who each stood as she approached them. As she approached their mother, Elizabeth started to stand up, but the family friend bent over and gave her an exceptionally long hug, and a few tears came from both of their eyes. After standing up again, the friend paused and placed a hand on the casket before going ahead to the podium.

As she stepped up to the podium, she thought back to her years as a pastor in a small church with about the regular attendance as the number in this audience. She couldn't believe that she now taught several thousand people at several weekend services. Even though she had gotten used to speaking in front of much larger gatherings, speaking at this one had made her not as confident as she relived her past life in front of all of them. She sometimes found it hard to remember her earlier life. It seemed almost like a dream now that her present life was so different. Once again, she felt this was a God-given teaching moment.

"Wow! After listening to those comments about me, I wonder what they say when I am not around?" she started with a smile. "Good morning, I also welcome you all here today to honor Chris Baldwin who lived a remarkable life. God used Chris to work His plan and purpose on others, including me.

To those who do not know me, I am Pastor Candace Parker, also known as Candy to some. I am the senior pastor at Sun Valley Community Church which is near Los Angeles, California."

The crowd laughed spontaneously, both shocked at her presence and at her joke about herself. It was clear from Candace's perspective that some of the guests were probably uncomfortable with her presence and her story.

"Yes, I am the Candace who dated Chris in Los Angeles. We were practically living together, to say the least. I am OK with everything that was said here because all of that is true. I was very self-centered and thought everyone owed me something. So how did I go from being like the 'other woman' to a Senior Pastor and dear friends of Chris' family? This is truly the story of the power of God to change lives in ways unimaginable to the rest of us.

"Let me begin when Chris came back to Los Angeles. From the start, I could tell something was different with Chris. Instead of being a carefree personality, he seemed to be preoccupied. When I asked about it, he'd just say things are busy at work, and he was overwhelmed trying to catch up. But as time went by, he became even more distant. Even his promotion did not cheer him up.

"Finally, at dinner one night I just confronted him about it. What he said shocked me. He said he wanted to break up with me, quit his job, and move back to Chicago to try to salvage his marriage. I was furious. I was starting to think of a future with him, and he was just going to walk away.

"I asked him why, and what he said would eventually change the course of my life. He said that he believed God was telling him to go back to his family. He talked about praying about it and trying to listen to the Holy Spirit. At the time, I had no clue what he was talking about. I was out of sorts and didn't know what was happening. Chris talked about how his daughter Jennifer was positively influenced by her Christianity and how she had talked with Chris about her faith while he was at their home.

"At the time, I had no use for God and Christians, in general. I didn't know how to argue with Chris about God. Unbelievably, I could have handled it better if he was cheating on me rather than God talking with him! Well, before I knew it, Chris was gone, back in Chicago.

"We kept in touch infrequently, and he told me about re-marrying Elizabeth. Now I was the one feeling jealous and betrayed. I really had trouble dealing with our breakup. I mean it wasn't my first failed relationship, but it was the first one I lost to God. I just didn't understand this.

"Finally, I decided to consider Christianity by attending a church in my neighborhood. I talked with one of the pastors about what had happened to Chris. He started to explain what the scriptures said about my situation and about Jesus Christ. A couple of years later, I invited Christ into my life and was baptized.

"After that, my whole life started to look different. I wanted to do something else with my life and got interested in becoming a pastor. After graduating from a small Bible college in southern California, I became a pastor at a small church outside of Los Angeles. Through God's grace, the church became one of the larger ones in the area.

"As I said, Chris and I stayed in touch and became friends. I married a man who I met while I was studying to be a pastor. He is not a pastor, but an engineer who works for a large aerospace company. He and I met at the church we both attended.

"After about ten years, I invited Chris and his family to visit my church. From what I heard from Chris, Elizabeth wasn't all in but decided to go along. Well, we all had a good visit, and we started to see each other from time to time. I could go on and on about how my life changed because of Chris, but I will say I believe God used our ill-fated relationship to execute His plan and purpose for my life.

"My experience reminds me of the story of Joseph in the Old Testament. Near the end of the story Joseph declares that God used his brothers' sinful plans to complete His holy plan and purpose for Joseph's life. I believe God did this in my life and Chris' life. He used our selfish plans for a much better, selfless purpose."

With that, Candace stepped away from the podium and hugged Elizabeth again on her way back to her seat. Many in the audience were not sure what to make of Candace's comments. There were many whispers among the guests. Her comments made a big impression on many of them.

Pastor Jim Stone waited a couple of minutes for everyone to settle down and then stood up at the podium to conclude the service. He was not sure how his words would close the service, but he did believe the earlier talks supplied a great witness for all present.

"As you have heard, Chris led a remarkable life. His life affected the course of his family's lives and tens of thousands of lives in a church in southern California. One more thing I need to add is that Chris and his wife, Elizabeth, started and led a support group for couples considering divorce. Their work in this area is credited to saving hundreds of marriages over the past thirty years. They used their own experiences to help others avoid the mistakes they made.

"As the Apostle Paul said about David, I feel confident in saying about Chris that he had 'served God's purpose in his own generation.' Paul goes on to say that David, like Chris, was buried and his body decayed as will Chris' and the rest of us after we die. However, Paul goes on to say that Jesus, who God raised from the dead, did not see decay. This is the great Christian hope, although our bodies will decay, our spirit lives on forever for those who put their trust in Jesus Christ as their Lord and Savior.

"An often-occurring part of this church's service is asking people to give their lives to Jesus Christ. In Matthew 28:19, Jesus said, 'Therefore go and make disciples of all nations, baptizing them in the name of the Father and of the Son and of the Holy Spirit,' The Baldwin family requested that I offer an opportunity to any of you that have not committed their lives to Jesus Christ to do so at this service."

Pastor Jim went ahead to have all close their eyes and bow their heads. He then invited anyone who wanted to give their life to Christ to raise their hand. Following this, all who raised their hands were asked to look at him and repeat a prayer said by the pastor of committing their lives to Christ. After this, he told everyone to open their eyes, and he led a round of applause for those who committed their lives to Christ.

"I realize this may have seemed unusual for a funeral but what better time to consider our own personal salvation than at a funeral. I can't think of a better way to honor what God did in Chris's life. Let us now conclude this service with prayer.

"Lord, thank you for the life of Christopher Baldwin and the way you used him for your glory. You once again used ordinary people to complete your purpose and plan for each of us. We pray for your healing presence in the Baldwin family to help them trust in your promise of everlasting life for Chris and all who believe in your Son, Jesus Christ. Thank You for those who committed their lives to Christ today. Let the Holy Spirit that entered them change their lives to one that is Christ-centered.

Now Lord, be with all of us as we go out into the world to continue our lives in your service. In Jesus' name, we pray. Amen."

About the Author

Fred Smith has a Ph.D. in Aeronautics and Astronautics. He grew up in New England and now lives in the Midwest. He is married with three grown children and has several grandchildren. He worked in the aerospace industry his entire career and has been writing books as a creative outlet for over ten years.

The author can be contacted through his website, cfredericsmith. com. All proceeds the author receives from sales of *Unseen Hope* will be donated to charities.